The Silver Serpent

A Tale That Kills

By Jeremy Pesch

Contents

Foreword

This book captures the essence of the period that the Nameless Man spent in the famous Silver Serpent Akuan, a time critical in the Nameless Man's recent history, which I feel is deeply misunderstood by contemporary historians and critics. I wrote this short novel to set the record straight as I realized my previous account of these events glossed over this important happening. This is a reconstruction from what I could get out of Quinn during my wondrous travels with him while we journeyed to Port Winslow.

I wish to prove that my best friend is innocent of being an inhuman monster born to kill, then die, only to be reborn again to kill once more. I wish to prove in this account that the unknowable, unsearchable man with no face or cause, widely known as the Nameless Man, is in fact knowable. For here and in my previous novel, I shall give him a human face and reveal to all what he has always fought for. Quinn, my greatest friend, this one's for you.

Jest Di Blum

Chapter 1 - Not What We Are

Strike first and strike fast, for there are only two kinds of people: the quick and the dead.
—First Oath of the Silver Serpents

In all the Eighteen Kingdoms, which hold together like beacons of civilization in a bleak, backward world, there is no greater green jewel than the wide, stretching lands named Danneish. Beyond Danneish's bastions of civilization that lie between the forests of its rolling hinterlands is a small, remote village just south of the Oxeria River.

The village is a twenty days' hard trek from anywhere important. This particular village is so hard to find that when the loggers traveled there, they had to hire local guides, and even they got lost trying to locate it. This almost mystical village sits in a land known for its plentiful harvests and endless woodlands, and that's where our story starts: the one and only Parika' Te Mo, otherwise known as nowhere incarnate.

***

Quinn knelt in silent meditation at the edge of the swamp bile that crept up onto the rim of the crumbling embankment. He had been waiting for what felt like hours but, in reality, must have been much less. Quinn hated waiting; he hated being patient. Regardless, he soldiered on without a single word of complaint like a statue of a hero of another age, such was his way at the time.

Quinn opened his eyes as he heard a change in the soundscape of the quiet, swampy scene. He saw in the distance the subject of his chase, the lone man who ailed humanity with his humble existence. Or so Quinn assumed. He had to make sure first.

The man stood and paddled his shallow boat against the mud of the shallow swamp. The shadows from mangroves concealed his face in the darkness but did not hide his form from view.

He was lean but made fat by the many animal hides he wore, which he had skinned himself. Inside the shallow boat lay many other skinned animals, some as corpses, others as furs yet to be oiled correctly. Quinn could see that much for himself even half a fathom away, as was his way.

This man was like him, Quinn deduced, a hunter in a world filled with prey. Quinn's nerves tensed. His heart beat a little faster as he watched this man, this hunter by trade, paddle slowly toward him. This man whom the villagers of Parika' Te Mo all considered a strange yet harmless young hermit.

Unlike others, the hermit did not falter for a moment when he saw Quinn, a strange young man like himself with an unsheathed blade on the ground before him. Many would have been perturbed by the sight of such a striking figure, a well-built statue of seriousness with a permanently piercing gaze, waiting for them on shore. But not this strange young hermit, Quinn thought. Because a hunter is always unafraid of its prey.

When the hunter finally came to the small array of decomposing timbers called the dock, Quinn's presence had become so intimidating that the hunter decided not to venture from his small boat, finally heeding caution.

"Who are ya?" the hermit said with anger, slighted by the accusation he felt coming from Quinn. "What ya doing 'ere among the mud and nauseous fumes?"

"Are you the one I'm looking for?" Quinn said emotionlessly as he shut his eyes.

"Lookin' for? Who are ya to be lookin' for anybody?"

Quinn said nothing, not wishing to give away his intentions. He just opened his eyes to look at the young hermit's face, surprisingly clean considering his environment. Not even a speck of muddy water was on his many fur coats.

This blond-haired, blue-eyed hermit was exceptionally clean. Much more so than Quinn, who had bathed that morning for the first time in three days. Could it be related to his Gift? Quinn thought.

"What is your name, hunter?" Quinn asked.

"I'm not a hunta', I'm a trappa'."

"Is there a difference?"

"To me d'ere is."

"I do not follow. What difference exists between them?"

"A hunta' goes out of their way to kill. A trappa' only kills what comes to 'em. The difference between the two is night and day."

At this moment both Quinn and the man he had travelled so far to kill realized that despite their words on the subject, each knew what the other was. Regardless of what the hermit had to say, a hunter always recognizes another hunter, as the scent of their fear is different from that of their prey.

"Are you the one that lives in the swamps south of here?" Quinn said cautiously, trying to move the conversation along.

"Aye, not that it's ya business."

"Then you must be the man I seek. The man the villagers call Telli."

"Don't call me dat. Only my friends call me dat. I'm Telligood to you."

"Let me ask you this, trapper Telligood. You live in a part of the swamp so toxic, so foul, that only Voidlings dare venture into it. Your 'friends in the village say you only come out of it once or twice every month or so. If that is true, how do you sustain yourself? Where do you get fresh water?"

Telligood huffed and got angrier by the moment at Quinn's cold, questioning face. Like all those who live beyond conventional civilization in Danneish, he did not have the manner of an obedient serf but that of a fiercely independent man from the Danneishie wilds, one inclined to neither trust nor endure another's authority. Despite himself, he answered Quinn's question anyway, as he felt that Quinn would not leave him alone without an answer.

"Can't boil swamp water, so I get it from a nearby spring."

"A freshwater spring in the middle of a noxious swamp? Never heard of such a thing." Quinn pecked at the man's answer like a bird with a worm.

"All the water round here has to come from somewhere. There are much stranger happenings in dis world than a freshwater spring in d'ese parts."

Quinn, not taking the answer seriously, just looked at him with a piercing menace that beamed out of his dark green eyes. Quinn's short black hair waved in a slight breeze that jingled distant wind chimes in the village of Parika' Te Mo not far yonder.

Telligood, still standing in his small boat, continued locking eyes with Quinn. Each man not saying nor doing anything further. Waiting like they had all the time in the world for the other to make their next move.

"Fine. You've got me," said Telligood as he threw his paddle onto the green, murky swamp water in front of him, causing a splash. "I guess there is no point in pretending, you've already made up your mind about me."

Quinn noted an immediate change in the man the villagers called Telli. He straightened his posture. He talked in full words, not shortening them like many of the folk born around there.

Telligood ripped off a few fur coats and threw them onto the corpses of his prey in the boat.

"Who are you then?! Who have they sent to kill me?!" Telligood roared not with anger but with clear authority.

"I am Quinn. A probationary member of the Silver Serpent Akuan."

"You're one of the famous Silver Serpents?" The young man, who looked to be around Quinn's age, shook his head dismissively, his hands on his hips. "I'd be honored that they'd go so far as to send the best of the best after me, yet I am disappointed that they could only muster one of you." Telligood laughed to himself, mocking Quinn as he added, "Bells, they didn't even send the best of their number after me. Just the new recruit . . ."

Quinn didn't care what this man said about him; Telligood was going to be dead soon.

"Listen, probationary Serpent. I'm not like the others. I cannot stress that enough."

"That's what all the people in your position say."

"No, but it really is true. I am not like them other deviants. Not at all."

"And why is that?" Quinn said with deadly seriousness.

"Can I trust you, to tell you this?"

"I'm here to kill you. What do you think?"

"What I mean to say is, can I trust you enough to hear me out?"

"I haven't raised my blade to slay you yet, have I?" Quinn said. He couldn't stop twitching at the dagger hidden behind his back as he remained kneeling.

"The truth is, I don't have any offensive powers from the Gift. You know the real reason you are hunting me, new recruit? I can purify water. I can turn any liquid into fresh, potable water.

9

That's all. And yet because I was born with this simple, humble Gift—"

"Because you were born a mutant. Instead of turning their child over to the proper authorities, your parents chose to conceal your true nature from the world."

"I was the only son of a large estate. My parents were elderly. Had they passed, everything would have gone to our rivals and—"

"There is always justifiable reason, isn't there? To do wrong, to break the law of the land." Quinn said this more as an empathic statement than in judgment, although it did not come across that way.

The Gifted man shook his head, not wishing to give up on his plea to Quinn. Had he known Quinn's true identity as the Nameless Man, he would never have attempted such a foolish endeavor.

"Couldn't you forget about me? I mean nobody any harm. Haven't I proven that by being a recluse? The first son of a nobleman does not choose to live as a hermit in the middle of nowhere for no reason. Haven't my actions over these past five years proven me good? Or at the very least, able to be forgiven?"

Quinn had heard it all before. The soft wind died down. The man's point, although predictable, had been made. Quinn put his other hand behind his back and made the Akuan hand sign for execute.

In the next moment, a razor-tipped arrow flew out from concealment, jumping through the air between twisted trees and vines, having departed from seemingly nowhere. The hunter, sensing the projectile the moment he heard the bow crack in the silent swampy air, reached out a hand and produced from it a litany of violent blue flame that burned the incoming arrow to a crisp mid-flight.

The arrowhead still flew, but lacking the aerodynamics of its plumed shaft, fell like a pebble at the hunter's feet. Telligood, with violence in his eyes, pointed his open palm at a still-kneeling Quinn and roared, "Leave me be! Tell your unseen friend to let me leave here in peace, or their new recruit will be burned to a cinder! I'm warning you! Can't you see I wish to do no harm?!"

"I need not tell them anything," Quinn said softly to only himself. Quinn watched as two of his Silver Serpent brothers, who had been until this point well concealed in the reeds of the swamp, burst out of the water, giving Telligood the fright that would end his life.

Coming from both sides of the small boat at the same time, Quinn's Akuan brothers Tryan and Lichale pulled the man out of his small boat and into the dark water where his fire Gift could do nothing. They slashed and cut down the mutant with vicious efficiency, so fast you'd blink and miss it.

While young Telligood thrashed underwater unable to breathe, the pair stabbed him in a series of quick, unrelenting, unforgiving blows, creating more holes in his dying body than seemed necessary. But they had to make sure he would die and then stay dead.

Having held Telligood's body under the swampy water for a good minute, Quinn's Akuan brothers released their grasp. Quinn watched as the body floated to the surface in water that was now as pure and crystal clear as never before.

As the formerly concealed archer called Seppa (another of Quinn's Akuan brothers) ran up behind Quinn to join them, all watched in awe the final, defiant act of Telligood: what had been dirty was made clean by Gift power—the entire swamp was now clean a fathom in each direction.

"Bells, he purified the entire swamp before we did him in. The locals will be bloody happy. Perhaps he wasn't such a bastard after all," said the brown-haired, sleepy-eyed jokester named Tryan.

"He was a Caster. They are all bent on evil, rogue or not. Don't forget that for a second," Lichale said in his thick Orrianian accent, which turned each *S* into a *Z*.

Lichale left the water wiping blood off his hands, not feeling any pleasure for what they had just done. As the senior member of this temporary grouping at the age of thirty-five, he ordered, "Quinn, Tryan, you two carry the corpse into town. Make sure it's covered. We'll bury him in the local cemetery there. Seppa, you and I will take his trade goods and give them to villagers. They won't be pleased to see their strange friend dead. Even when they learn he was a Rogue Caster in their midst . . ."

As Quinn got up to help Tryan lug the corpse of the Rogue Caster Telligood out of what was now a crystal-clear lake, Quinn concluded his conversation with the dead man in his head. He said to him, *My fellow hunter, there is no forgiveness under the law. Only guilt and prices paid. In this world of fleeting life and impending death, there is no room in my heart for forgiveness, for mercy, for murderers like you.*

#

The four rank-and-file men of the famous Silver Serpent Akuan had gotten their man, had won their game of hunter and prey. Yet none of them felt any better for it. The faces of the villagers of Parika' Te Mo didn't make them feel any better either. Quinn and Tryan dragged the wrapped body of Telligood through the muddy street that lay between fortified dwellings and storage shacks made of rotting timbers and thatched roofs.

Women sobbed openly for Telligood, falling to their knees in despair for the strange young man they had once called their friend. Even some of the men shed a tear for the kind hermit they had grown to know and care for over the last half decade.

12

Lichale and Seppa presented to the locals what the dead man had left behind as a kind of apology for what the Silver Serpents had done. Even if it was lawful, from the villagers' perspective, the Serpents had not only killed their friend but also cut off a good source of furs and meats that the village relied upon. The locals would not let themselves be seen receiving this gift, although they likely took possession of it later out of necessity.

For although the villagers of Parika' Te Mo were as poor as they come, they were still rich with pride and good conscience. If a lawman comes and kills your friend righteously, you do not then take any pleasure in said executioner's acquaintance, do you? The villagers shared that sentiment, as they now saw the Silver Serpents as they truly were—executioners.

Despite all this. Despite the despair, despite the many villagers of the town following the procession of Silver Serpents to the overgrown cemetery in silent protest (a cemetery that looked like it was haunted, even in direct daylight). Despite all the crying and carrying on, not one voice let out any anger at the Silver Serpents.

The man whom the prideful but saddened villagers watched Quinn, Tryan, Seppa, and Lichale dig a grave for and bury was but a Caster of supernatural Gifts and, even worse, a rogue one. A man of the small percentage of humanity born with the Gift of the Void, which is widely claimed to corrupt one's very soul.

Casters are known as an ugly spot, a blemish that is only tolerated in society by gathering them all into organizations that the public can then openly condemn. This man had chosen a life of seclusion to avoid that; he had gone rogue.

That is one sin that can never be forgiven. No matter the religion, culture, or creed. No matter what. For that is what the majority have decreed and what remains to this day. For better or worse, the prey have decided that the hunters of this world, called Terranova, should be hated and, at worst, openly slain.

I shall close this first chapter of this account I will be calling *The Silver Serpent* with something that Quinn once heard his Akuan brother Lichale say, much later after this terrible—yet just—killing. At the campfire, late into the cold night after a few pints of warm ale, he said, "This whole morality business, it's not an Akuansman's job. It's not any of our concern who is right and wrong here. You know how I know it isn't? If it was, we'd get paid far better than we do now. That's for sure. You see the villagers here see us as executioners, but that isn't right. We aren't the executioner; we are the executioner's blade. Honestly, that's all an Akuan is, a weapon pointed at the various enemies of humanity. Sadly, that means we don't get to choose who we slay."

Chapter 2 – A Bar Fight but with Words

While Quinn and his Akuan brothers hunted Telligood, the rest of the Akuan, excluding their commander and second adjunct, came to a building in Parika' Te Mo that could be mistakenly called a pub. There they were going to listen to a tall tale if ever there was one. At least according to the bartender that day, whom I recently interviewed for this part of the account. I shall not name him here as he wishes to remain anonymous. He wants his quiet life to stay that way.

While Quinn may not be present for this part of the story, I've included it anyway as it's nonetheless important to know. For every fantastical quest to slay a monster starts with a legend, with a tall tale told.

***

Rugged men that formed the other half of the Silver Serpents Akuan entered the public house in good cheer, smelling like swamp water and sweat. The patrons and staff of the public house would have been offended by such a stench had they not smelt much the same.

The group of five sat in the center of the modest public room at a table made out of the untimely remains of a wooden hand cart, which seemed as though it had sunk and been left in the swamp for far too long. No, one would not rightly label this public house, the Pothole to locals, a pub. It was more a collection of broken items contained within a house that always leaked water from its roof, even on a clear summer's day.

It was here the Serpents came, loud and proud in the mostly silent establishment, and started their little celebration after a hard morning's labor.

"Red, it's your turn to buy a round," said Gus, a big-boned man as he liked to call himself. He'd struggled during his Akuansman's career against a well-earnt beer belly.

"Ya havin' a laugh, mate. It's Michael's turn," the red-haired man named Red said as the five sat down on rather uncomfortable small wooden stools and a single upside-down bucket.

"No, it ain't," the tight-lipped Michael said as he kept his hood on, covering much of his scarred face.

"Bryon, lad, that leaves you," Gus said to the biggest in stature of all five men there, the dumb giant called Bryon. Tryan's unidentical twin.

"Na, mate, I covered it last time. And the time before. On ya horse." Bryon flipped his chin in the direction of the door, indicating to his Akuan brother that he should, as the regular folk put it delicately, go jump.

Samson, a handsome man, even late into his fifties, laughed at his Silver Serpent brothers' banter as he gestured to the bartender that this round was on him.

"Come, lads, who cares about money? We are here to celebrate and celebrate we shall!" Samson roared. He then took a bloody sack from his belt and, after it thudded heavily on the table, unwrapped its contents for all to see.

It was the gray-beaked head of a Graypecker. A very rare, very dangerous Voidling beast said to be the Void-corrupted offspring of geese, of all things. However, Graypeckers, as those unlucky few who have seen them know, do not look anything like geese. While they stand on two webbed feet and have a long neck with a beak on its head, they also have the stature of an ostrich, as well as the land speed of a racehorse and the cunning of a particularly crafty fox. There's also their ability to fly to contend with.

A disastrous bit of alien nature to grace our unfortunate world, to be sure. That these five Akuansmen managed to find its swampy lair and then overcome its acid-spitting ways to kill it was a small yet noteworthy event worthy of celebration. And so the Silver Serpents carried on with loud cheers at the mere sight of it. However, the other patrons of the small establishment didn't see it that way.

"You lot, keep it down over there! An old man is trying to tell some young'uns an important tale."

While the bartender put a round of drinks on their table, First Adjunct Samson turned around on his bucket-made-stool to look at the three other patrons in the public house, a number which was relatively high for a small village establishment well before the midday meal.

"I apologize, my good man, for my men and I's emotive conduct. We shall endeavor to be more courteous from now on," Samson said effortlessly in his charismatic nature, which totally disarmed the old man, who appeared to be ten years older than but was actually around the same age as Samson.

"Ya havin' a good yarn over there, are ya? Speak up. We like to know important stories too," Gus said aloud to the three locals at the back wall of the public house, who seemed to have been nursing their pints for as long as possible in order to have reason to stay indoors on that cold but sunny day.

"Yeah, I like stories. Speak up, elder, so we can all hear," added Bryon as the sentiment carried through the rest of the five Akuansmen.

Enjoying being the center of attention, the old man came to the bar with his two young friends in tow. He was more than happy to tell people his tale, as he thought it was one everyone everywhere should know.

"I'm Pell. This here is Dip and Lazy Eye. We all of Parika' Te Mo," said the old man before the Serpents.

"Born and raised," said Dip with pride.

"Lazy Eye? Why's he called that?" said Bryon, speaking before thinking as was his usual manner of communication.

"Because he's missing a foot! Why do ya think he's called that?! You moron," said Gus to a now understanding Bryon.

Old man Pell cleared his throat as Samson ordered three new pints of beer for their thankful new acquaintances. On his own tab, of course.

"What I shall tell you now, lads, shall strike fear into your very soul. For many a brave man and woman have fought the Void and its foul creations before. But none like this. None before have encountered the foul creature that is the villain of the story I shall tell you now. None, I dare say, have ever suffered this fresh horror of the Void."

***

Beyond the nauseous swamps around Parika' Te Mo and into the Deep Woods, where none of even the highly trained Danneishie Forest Rangers dare to go, lies a dark place yonder from which none who venture ever return. Ya see, it all started six months ago when a cloud of evil descended over our fair village and then travelled northeast toward those Deep Woods. It was a purplish-black cloud that came and went during the midday meal. Dip and Lazy Eye, you two both saw it, didn't ya? By the Saints, we all did.

Ever since that descending cloud of darkness passed us overhead like an ill omen of old, strange happenings have been afoot. Birds falling from the sky, struck dead by unknown forces. Potatoes and other vegetables rotting in the ground just before harvest. Deer killed by hunters in the neighboring areas have been brought back and, when butchered, revealed to be carrying a mess of Void parasites within instead of their internal organs.

Worse still, any Forester that ventures deep into the forest groves comes back turned as a fully mutated Biter, claws, fangs, and all. Bells, they even think Debbie's daughter's disappearance has somthin' to do with what's been happening here of late.

It's not only the locals that this curse is affecting. An expedition of the Logging Guild went into the Deep Woods about a month and a half back. They were searching for a new source of stoa oak for markets abroad, the nobleman said. We've heard nothin' from them since. Nor the armed search party of Gavidor mercenaries that went after them just a week ago. Nay, actually that ain't true. Some of them did return, undead and corrupted, just like the many others. Some of the young lads like Dip and Lazy Eye here had to band together like an Akuan would to put them all down for good and protect this village.

Yes, all the evidence is there. Something foul has befallen our lands, our backyard, I tell ya. Unlike most, I know why. I know the real reason behind all this. You see, in the Deep Woods there have always been Voidlings. Since the time of my grandfather's grandfather, Akuans have been hunting those horrors there. That is not new. But what is is the new Voidling that has taken up residence there. Very mysterious.

It has its many eyes on Parika' Te Mo, ya see. It wants our village for itself, and so it tries to scare us off the lands of our ancestors. But none here are so intimidated, despite all its maniacal attempts to have at us!

Surely these terrible happenings shall continue here should this villain, this foul creature, remain. Everyone has said it, there can be no coexistence with this entity. It must not be endured any longer; it must be slain. But for that, it would mean a band of heroes brave enough to venture into said Deep Woods and slay it. We've tried to summon such a band, but though word has gone out, none have come.

Worse still, it is also said that the being cannot be harmed by conventional means, that it is like a spirit or ghost which can take possession of a host whenever it wishes and thus is immortal. But there is still hope.

For there have been whispers among the local Lore Masters and Forest Rangers that know the Deep Woods and the Voidlings there well. There may still be a way to slay this terrible fiend once and for all.

I've heard from them that only the one who knows the truth of the Deep Woods shall undo the curse that has befallen Parika' Te Mo. That only those in search of the truth shall be able to find and slay the monster responsible for all our woes. What truth is that? Not even the Lore Masters know. What words have meaning enough to slay what is most likely a fully sentient Voidling? One which has shown itself to be as clever and devious as we are. That, who can even bloody guess?

What's it look like, you ask? What does this sentient Voidling take as its form when not ethereal? Well, there is much confusion about that. Some say it looks like a small human child. Others who claim to have seen it say it looks like a large spider with the teeth of a man instead of fangs. Others say it is like a rainbow-colored bird that has no head but many eyes on the underside of its larger-than-a-house wingspan. Nobody knows for sure. In fact, the only thing we are sure about is that we are forbidden to say its true name aloud on pain of curse. Thus, we all call it the Forbidden One.

***

The five Serpents, having heard Pell's story, were silent for a moment while each processed the many details of his account. It wasn't often, but sometimes a tall tale heard in a public house like this had at least a kernel of truth to it. However, on this occasion, the five Silver Serpents, monster hunters by trade, found not even that much. Regardless of their silence, Pell continued anyway.

"Actually, now I'm thinkin' on it, perhaps all we need is a famous Akuan like yours to do something meaningful about it. No other Akuan has taken our village head's contract, perhaps you lot will?"

The Silver Serpents looked at each other with a smile. The dubious details of this far-fetched tale were probably the reason no other Akuan took up this contract. Despite the reasonable reward offered for such a perilous task, no Akuan in their right mind would trek into the famously deadly Deep Woods to find a likely fictional sentient Voidling that the locals couldn't even describe properly.

"Thank you for the kind offer, but I think we'll have to pass on this contract," Samson said kindly as he tried to distract from some of his fellow Serpents who were laughing at the thought of taking it up.

"What? You think slaying the Forbidden One is beneath ya? Do you lot only kill Casters or somethin'?" said Dip, feeling slighted that the Serpents weren't taking the story seriously.

"No, what Samson was politely sayin' was that while your story was mildly entertaining, it doesn't fakkin' make any sense," said Gus, his arms crossed over his belly, his pint empty from before the story even started.

Dip, feeling offended, put down his pint and walked up to the table. It was then that the bartender realized how weak to liquor young Dip was. He was drunk. Gus, the famous pub brawler, not caring about that fact, stood up, ready to knock the man onto his arse if he needed to.

Sensing trouble brewing, the ever-diplomatic Samson stood up and got between the two men, one a drunk boy, the other a battle-hardened, sell-sword warrior.

"Now, now, lads, let's settle this difference of opinion with words, not fists. Let us Serpents explain to you what, by your story, is really happening here."

Both men returned to where they had been sitting upon hearing Samson's naturally calming voice. Samson sat down and laid it out straight.

"Pell, you've made many interesting claims, which are first-person accounts, I grant you that. But the conclusions you've come to are simply wrong. The events you've described as evidence of a curse can almost all be independently explained."

"How so?" Pell said, feeling slightly offended.

"First of all, of course the bloody Logging Guildsmen got killed hunting for what is effectively tree gold. As you've implied, only Akuans and Rangers dare venture into the Deep Woods. That is for a fakkin' good reason. You need to understand the Void well to have any hope of going that far into the unknowns," said Gus.

"The search party probably died because their mercenaries were shite," added Bryon after a sip of his pint.

"Gavidor mercenaries are known to be a bunch of limp-wristed fighters that only get hired because they are so cheap. Of course they died quick," said Red as a statement of fact.

"The vegetables rotting in the soil is likely due to it being extra damp around here due to the late rainy season," Samson explained.

"Deer filled with Voidling parasites? That's probably Chikrains that you're talking about. If enough of them are inside an animal's body, they can take full control of it, even act as the animal's digestive track. Uncommon but not unheard of," added the quiet-in-demeanor Michael, who was the Akuan's surgeon, the only member of their Akuan with a university degree.

"Debbie's child, I'm sorry to say, was found by two of our number just this morning. It looks like she fell into the out-of-use well just outside of town, and nobody had thought to look for her there until now," Samson said soberly.

"Then what about the descending cloud we all saw? What is your explanation for that? What about the birds falling from the sky for no reason?" Pell asked desperately, offended that his story was coming apart at the seams. To those two questions, however, the Serpents were quiet, as they could not easily explain them away.

"It's just another couple UVEs," Gus eventually said.

"A UVE?" Pell said, still feeling indignant.

"It's Akuan speak for Unknown Void Event. There's no rhyme or reason to 'em," explained Red.

"Wait a second. If nobody ever says the Forbidden One's name because it brings a lifelong curse on ya, then how does anyone ever learn it? Are you allowed to write it down or somethin'?" Bryon said in a rare moment of brilliance.

As soon as the old man's eyes hit the floor, the Serpents knew the truth for themselves. This story was fiction; the Forbidden One didn't exist. The old man turned his back on the Serpents as he stood at the bar without a word. Gus, Red, and Bryon then openly laughed.

"Not much of a story, I tell ya. All the good ones have at least a little bit of truth in them to make them good," Gus said.

"Still, it's interesting to hear the kind of nonsense cooked up by the imaginative minds that live here," Red said with laughter.

"I think these lads have been staring at the swamp water for far too long," said Bryon in his dumb seriousness, which caused even Michael to smirk.

"Tone it down, lads. We are guests here; act like it," said Samson the authority figure in a fatherly tone.

"Oh, ha-ha-ha. You lot think ya so bloody tough. That you know everything there is to know about the Void. But you ain't know shit compared to those that live near the edges of it," said the previously quiet young man in his twenties called Lazy Eye.

"What do you know, kid, about fighting the Void?" asked Gus from his proverbial high horse. Lazy Eye stepped up to the Silver Serpent's table.

"It seems I know more than you lot. As I am smart enough to see Pell's tale as the truth it is," Lazy Eye said with an expression of great seriousness, despite the added comical element of his left eye's pupil wandering away.

"You seem to have a superiority complex, eh lad? Let's take this outside, and I can fix it for you," said Gus intimidatingly, as he felt he had no time for showboating fools such as the one before him. Lazy Eye, feeling the sense of immortality known only to young, foolish men, did not back down for a second, even with a brotherhood of deadly Caster killers before him.

"Have you ever killed anybody, Serpent?" Lazy Eye said in ignorance.

"Is water fakkin' wet?" Gus said as he stood up with a pissed off expression.

"Easy lads," Samson curtailed.

"Seriously, Gus, must you fight every loudmouth bastard we come across?" Michael added as Gus and Lazy Eye stood eye to eye with each other, like a pair of bare-knuckle boxers trying to intimidate one another before a prizefight.

"To be honest, I planned on doing ya in from the moment you walked in here. You are loud, obnoxious, and ugly. You remind me of my deadbeat father. He was a pussy as well," Lazy Eye said with menace before he peacocked by taking off his shirt right there and then, exposing his well-built muscles, earned through a laborer's life in a swampy, dangerous land.

"You wanna fight? You've got it, you daft idiot. You know what they say, lads, everyone's got a plan until they get punched

24

in the face," Gus said as he took off his forest-green Silver Serpent cloak and started winding up his right hook.

Before violence could ensue, Red, Bryon, and Michael jumped off their stools to hold back the raging torrent that was Gus, preventing the famous pub brawler from removing all the teeth from the young man's jaw in a single blow.

Dip, Pell, and Samson rushed to hold back Lazy Eye as the men yelled colorful insults at each other.

"I'll eat ya for breakfast, old man!" roared Lazy Eye.

"I'm gonna fakk you! Then when I'm done, I'm gonna fakk ya mother!" said Gus unnecessarily colorfully.

"Serpents, to attention!" yelled the former Sergeant Fredstar out of nowhere, interrupting the scene of descending chaos. All the men turned to look at the doorway where two new figures now stood. The Serpents stood at attention immediately when they saw Second Adjunct Fredstar behind their Akuan Commander Tar.

Seeing the reverence that the five Serpents had for this strange old man, who was well into his seventies, even Lazy Eye, Dip, and Pell stood up straight.

"Who's dat?" said Dip to Pell quietly.

"That, I think, is their commander, Tar. He is said to be the greatest expert on the Void in Danneish. Perhaps even the world," Pell said quietly back.

Tar came into the center of the public house slowly, without a word to or from anyone. He went over to Gus, who had his head down, looking at the hay-covered floor in shame. Then Tar looked at Lazy Eye, whom he had never seen before. Tar stopped his long inspection of the men and then stood before Samson, the Akuan's first adjunct, Tar's second-in-command.

"What is this then, Sammy?" Tar asked in his accentless voice, which he had earned by being fluent in many languages.

25

"A minor disagreement, sir. About a tall tale told," said Samson to his commander.

"It's not a tall tale. It's the truth!" said Lazy Eye. Tar walked over to the man, who stood tall but not as tall as he was.

"What's the tale about, young one? Do I already know it?" he said as he commanded all eyes in the room easily with his natural sense of authority, as was his usual manner.

"We was talking about the Forbidden One, sir," Lazy Eye said, quickly losing his sense of youthful bravado.

Tar stepped away from the lot of them as he nodded his head in agreement, probably to just himself. He walked to the doorway, and before he went through it, he turned to them still at attention, then said, "Come on then. There is a curse on this town and a Voidling to slay to lift it. Worse still, me thinks we Serpents are the only ones who can pull off said nonsense."

The men of the Silver Serpents, excluding Fredstar, were flabbergasted by this unexpected news.

"But, sir, how can any of this story be true? Voidlings, even sentient ones, go around killing people, not cursing them," said Samson in place of all his brothers.

To this, Tar simply said, "I admit, there is a strangeness attached to this new Voidling, more so than we have ever encountered before. But regardless, it is a problem that needs a solution, and we are all these people have. There will be no time for reinforcements, other Akuans to join in this new campaign against the Void. All we have to muster is ourselves. Let us hope we are more than enough."

Chapter 3 – The One That Got Away

Not much is known about the fair damsel who went by the strange name that is Sae. I admit that when I had put my mind to telling this tale, I searched the many roads, villages, and taverns of Danneish to find any trace of Quinn's long-lost lover. I wished to meet her, for one. Quinn always had a habit of drawing the good-looking, dangerous types to him, and two, I wished to get her side of the story that is the complicated man called Quinn. The third objective in my small list was to confirm if that was her real name, as I suspect it wasn't.

However, in my many travels, I did not meet even one person who knew her or had even seen a woman matching her exact description. The only reason I know that she even existed outside of Quinn's memory is because my fellow Laughing Heart Akuan member Groose had met her numerous times. As she used to follow the Silver Serpents around like a little sister who was their unofficial thirteenth member.

Other than the fact that she and Quinn courted for a time during his probationary period within the Silver Serpent Akuan, I'm afraid we know nothing of her. So instead of Sae's recount of what happened between her and Quinn among the many bog-riddled swamps of Parika' Te Mo, I shall instead share what I managed to wrangle out of Quinn's memory of that day using some of my good old-fashioned nagging.

Quinn dared not speak much of her at all, you see, in the way a scorned lover wishes not to speak of their painfully departed. But I got this much from him—the manner in which they forever parted ways.

***

It was afternoon, after all the Serpents had their modest lunch of swamp fish soup and cabbage bread, when they gathered in the cemetery of Parika' Te Mo. It was there, not too far from where Telligood had been buried that morning, that they stood and sat among the many graves of the long since departed.

In the haunting shadows of trees that caressed the many weatherworn tombstones lay another recently dug grave. One which was smaller than most as it was the grave of a child. In particular, it was meant for Debbie's drowned daughter, whom Tryan and Bryon had the unfortunate luck to stumble upon that very morning as Quinn and his other Akuan brothers dealt with Telligood.

"Are we really going to do this? It doesn't seem right . . ." said Seppa as he itched his dark skin, which was covered in mosquito bites. The uneasy sentiment carried by his words was reflected through the crowd of all eleven Silver Serpents gathered, plus the extra, the unofficial one more.

"You boys are crazy. Absolutely crazy. Does being in an Akuan also drive you mad?" said Sae as she rested her head against Quinn's upper arm. Her red hair was as dark as blood and fell easily around her shoulders.

"Fakk, I left behind my sanity long ago," Gus mumbled as he and Lichale jumped down into the recently dug grave to bring out the child-sized coffin within. The very one that the town's carpenter had made that morning out of a few discarded timbers from a dilapidated shack, half sunken into the swamp not far from the village center.

Once Gus and Lichale had picked up the grave's contents and then slid the coffin beside the grave, Tryan wrestled with his seven-inch-long finishing dagger to pop the nailed-shut coffin lid open. The rest of the Silver Serpents crowded around it so all could see the dusty-haired little girl about seven or eight years of age within, now wearing the blue, pale face of death.

Gus and Lichale jumped out of the grave as Quinn heard Debbie and her husband cry to themselves as they left the graveyard limits and went back toward their home, which would now be forever emptier than before. It was clear to all that while what the Silver Serpents were doing was necessary, it was in no way desired. Still they soldiered on, for they had a village to save, a monster to slay.

"Well, she's dead alright. Although I could have told you that from just the smell," said Tryan as he held his nose. Tar, the orchestrator of this uncovering of the dead, looked up and down the body of the small child, which was still somewhat bloated from being waterlogged in a well for a few days, then nodded his head in approval.

"Yes . . . this one will do," he said coldly, as if he was not looking at the corpse of a child but an instrument to be used. "Nail the coffin back up. We'll take it as is."

Quinn looked at Sae's cold, calculating face. Through her tight-lipped expression, Quinn could tell that his woman wasn't happy. She rarely was okay with the dangerous risks the Akuan life forced Quinn to take. That this most recent endeavor was starting with a morally dubious act likely stressed her concerns. Concerns that Sae was always in the habit of voicing.

"So . . . let me get this straight," Sae said as Samson threw Tryan a hammer so he could put the coffin's lid back on. "You boys are going to bring the corpse of this child into the Deep Woods so that when you meet this Forbidden One all the locals are on about, you can force it into this child's body and then kill it once and for all?"

"Precisely," said Tar as he peered with dark green eyes at Sae, who was still hanging off Quinn's arm.

"By the Saints, when you put it that way, it really does start to seem crazy," said Red as he smoked his tobacco pipe while sitting on a nearby tombstone.

"What would be more crazy, more morally wrong, as I see it, would be to turn our backs and leave this village and its people to suffer under this Voidling's curse," said Second Adjunct Fredstar, a man in his fifties like Samson but of foreign Suddran heritage like Seppa, which was made apparent by his dark skin.

"Sometimes it takes crazy to fight crazy. Remember that, lads, when fighting the Void," said First Adjunct Samson as he scratched his white beard.

"Well, we must have a pretty big advantage then. As this plan has got to be up there with the craziest I've heard. Which lot of Voidling-killing bastards came up with this horrifying technique? Using a corpse like this . . . I've never heard of it before," said Michael.

"I did." Tar smiled as he claimed sole credit. "This is my crazy, lads, my crazy."

A few of the Serpents chuckled as they were all very much used to Commander Tar's off-kilter nature by now. As it was exactly how Samson put it that day, to become a worthy adversary of the Void, one must first be a little mad, a little crazy. That, the well-respected Voidling expert Tar definitely was.

"Lads, I reckon I know what kind of sentient Voidling the Forbidden One is. I believe it is a Body Snatcher. A Rellian is its scientific name. And if I'm right, my plan will definitely see its end." Tar kicked the coffin for emphasis.

"Sir, with all due respect, what if we are wrong about this? What if there really is no curse like some of us first thought?" said Seppa, always the doubter, speaking his mind before them all.

"Yeah, what if it's a load of bollocks, sir? I really don't wanna see whatever horrors lurk in the Deep Woods," said Bryon, who, while very proud of being an Akuansman, was always unenthusiastic to do the work of one.

"If the Forbidden One is made-up, that will become apparent before we even reach the Deep Woods. If nothing strange happens on the way over there, we shall turn back and have confirmed it all a tall tale indeed. Sadly though, I don't think that is the way this shall play out," Tar said with his old-wise-man smile, which reassured his men a little.

"Bells, I've made it through thirty-two years of life without having to venture into the Deep Woods once. I guess I'm going to be breaking that streak," said Lichale in quiet despair as it started to spit rain overhead and the wind picked up, moving the many branches of trees into a side-to-side dance around them.

"It shall be a first for us all, excluding Tar, of course," Quinn said in agreement with his brothers. Tar then shot a smile at him. For while Quinn did not know this at the time, not even Tar in all his seventy-four years, of which forty were spent in the Silver Serpent Akuan, had ever been into that foul, Voidling-infested hellhole called the Deep Woods. This risky venture to lift a curse, to save a people by the use of a child's corpse, would be a first for them all. I dare say, even a first for this world's history books as well.

***

Soon after the graveside meeting, the Silver Serpents made preparations to leave Parika' Te Mo on foot. Their journey would take them three days one way, without use of their horses, as the terrain would only get more difficult from here on and thus only travel on foot could be achieved. It was then, when Quinn was tying up the Akuan's horses at Parika' Te Mo's only sheltered stable, that the beginning of the end started—as he would later say. The beginning of the end of Sae and him. It started with only five words from her.

"Do you have a moment?"

Quinn finished tying up the last of the Akuans' eleven horses to the back wall of the mostly enclosed stable. Even if it should rain heavily tonight, the horses should stay dry here, he thought.

"I don't have much time now, but okay. Tar wants us all back at the graveyard soon with all that good sense would have us carry. We are packing light—going to be mostly living off the land for the next week or so," Quinn said, half distracted by his mare in front of him.

"I'm not going with you," Sae said bluntly. Her usual girlish freckled smile was not present. Nor had it been for the last few days, Quinn remembered.

"That's fine. Actually, I was hoping you'd stay here in Parika' Te Mo and wait until we return. It shouldn't be more than a week."

Sae huffed at Quinn's remark. Clearly, she had not forgotten their argument from two weeks before. She smiled falsely as she said, "I thought we already talked about this. I'm not the type of person who waits patiently in the background for others, for her 'hero' to come home."

Quinn, the stoic-looking man she had let herself fall for, started to brush his horse as he said, "Nor the type brave enough to come with us, it seems."

"How dare you say that? I've followed you boys around most of Danneish. Through thick and thin, I've been with you. Not once have I run away or even cowered. Even when we fought the Demikiny or the various Rogue Casters we found along the way. You can't call me a coward now, my love. You know me. I'm not someone who runs away."

32

"I know. It's one of the reasons I like you so much." Quinn looked at her with a smile that took her off the offensive, just for a moment.

"No . . . I'm not a coward. I'm a realist. One who sees no realistic way that this plan of Tar's is going to work."

Quinn stopped brushing his mare. He came around his horse to face her properly, his face showing clearly that he wanted her to elaborate. Sae took Quinn's two hands in hers, her fingers small in comparison.

"My love, what I say next must stay between you and me. You and me only. Understood?" Sae asked gently. Quinn reluctantly nodded with a serious expression, which many often felt intimidated by. "I can't tell you how I know this. So you are going to have to trust me. Tar's wrong. It isn't a body snatcher that has cursed this village. It's something much, much worse."

"You know what it is? But how?" said Quinn with visible confusion. How does this everyday Danneishie, a tavern waitress when he met her, know something about the Void that even the great Voidling expert Tar doesn't know? he thought.

"Again, my love, I can't tell you how I know. Only that it's not going to work. That child's corpse will be useless when you go before it."

"Do you know what it really is then?"

"I do."

"Then tell me. Better yet, tell Tar—"

"I can't do that," Sae said, cutting Quinn off as she tore her hands from his.

"But why?"

"Because then I would need to tell you how I know what it is. And that is something, my love, that I can never tell you or him."

33

"Why?" Quinn said with deadly seriousness. His patience with Sae having run out, he grabbed her gently by the shoulders. "Sae, if there is a greater threat here than would appear to both me and my brothers, you must tell us. Or at least tell me what it truly is."

"I can't. If I tell you what it is, you'll try to go with them and kill it. But whether you know what it is or not will not change the outcome, Quinn. I hate to be a doomsayer, but it's the truth. All who go to slay the Forbidden One will never return. Your brothers are going to their deaths with this mission of Tar's . . . I can't stand the thought of you going with them," Sae said, suggesting that desertion from the Akuan was the only way forward for them.

Quinn was shaken by his lover's words. In that moment, a battle erupted within him in which his loyalty to his Akuan brothers was pitted against his loyalty to her.

"Again, I ask you. How do you know these things? How are you so certain of the end result?"

Sae looked up at Quinn, into his eyes, as she shed a lone tear. "That, my love, I think you already know . . ."

Quinn released her from his grasp as Sae confirmed with a tear what he had always suspected about her in the back of his mind. Sae was a Rogue Caster, one who was hiding in the shadow of an Akuan that specialized in the hunting of Rogue Casters, just as Quinn was.

For the Nameless Man was none other than the most famous Rogue Caster this world has ever known. Had his fellow Silver Serpents known on that rainy afternoon that two Rogue Casters were in their midst, Quinn and Sae would have been slain just as Telligood was by the men who called themselves the executioner's blades. Just as the law of the land required and proclaimed.

Quinn, not wishing to admit to Sae that he was as she was, a hunter in the clothing of prey, said nothing. He backed away from her and looked down at his feet.

"So, you really did know all this time . . . Yet you said nothing to the others," Sae said. She wiped the lone tear off her cheek, and her expression grew colder, more serious.

"I didn't know for sure until now," Quinn said, not daring to look at her.

"Will you tell your brothers?"

"No," Quinn said after a short while.

"Will you come with me then? Will you escape this suicide mission to the depths of Void-induced hell?"

"What about the people here?" Quinn looked up from the ground to see her freckled face made evil-looking by the shadows of the dark stable.

"They will all die regardless. There is a noose tightening around this village. Once it's brought to tension, there will be no escape, even should they attempt to flee when it gets desperate here. By then, it'll be too late. If we don't leave here together within the next few hours, we won't be able to escape that same fate."

Quinn was shocked by her selfishness, the callousness of this woman he thought he had known so well. It was as if he had grown to know another person until now, a fake image of a woman he thought he could love. Or so it seemed in that fleeting moment. She looked up at him with her cold, blue, determined eyes.

"Well, my love, what is your answer? Will you come with me? Will you save yourself from the tragedy that is playing out before us?"

"How can you say all this without even a look of sadness on your face?" Quinn shook his head in disbelief. "You've been with the Silver Serpents almost as long as I have. They all count

35

you as their little sister and dote on you when they can. Yet you don't seem to care an iota for them. It's like you no longer have any use for them, so you are willing to discard them at a moment's notice. I wonder, if I went with you now, perhaps there would be a day when I too proved inconvenient enough to be abandoned as well."

"Quinn, I would never—"

"You would never? Why? What makes my life more special than theirs?" Seeing that she had an answer but would not speak it to him, Quinn said something to her that he'd regret for a lifetime. "I love the Silver Serpents more. Do you realize that? By getting me to pick between you and my brothers, by not telling me what I really need to know in order to slay the Forbidden One, I dare say you actively help it. You are willing to let all these people here die? I am not. I am not selfish enough to do so. Where is the woman I grew to love?"

Sae slapped Quinn across his face. It was as hard as a punch. It left a red handprint on his face well into the evening.

"I'm sorry I had to slap you," she said, not sorry at all, as Quinn recovered from the blow. "But no words can convey to you the blow you just dealt me. To say I'm in any way complicit in this is stupid and juvenile," said Sae, purposefully evading Quinn's allegations.

"You act like all these people here are already dead, and still you do not cry for them!" Quinn said with heated emotion.

"I'm *sorry* I don't look sad enough for you, that I'm too good at hiding my own pain and melancholy for you to see my crying on the inside at all this. But please, you idiot, understand that while I may be a Caster, while I may be powerful due to my mutations, even I have limits on my abilities. On the choices I can make, to who I can and cannot save. I can only save one person here from this cursed tragedy. That being you. But now that you've said how you really feel, I'm not sure I want to anymore!" Sae turned on her heel, then started to throw a saddle on her horse.

"Sae, Sae, wait," Quinn pleaded as he watched her ready her horse and ignore him.

"I'm sorry for what I said. I didn't mean it to come out that way. I know you still care," Quinn said as she untethered her horse from the stable's anchor point. "Please. Can we not talk about this?"

"What is there to talk about?" Sae got up on her horse. "You've chosen them over me."

"What were you expecting? You are courting an Akuansman. It's a job, a profession for a lifetime . . . The only way to quit is through death or eternal dishonor."

"Remember, Quinn, you aren't one of them yet. I was expecting you to feel the same way I do. That you are better off with me than with them." She looked down at him from her horse. She was beyond upset.

"Sae, please. Don't leave like this. Let us talk more. About the Forbidden One . . . About you and me. We can work this out, I'm sure," Quinn pleaded, pained at the thought of her leaving in a rage because of his careless words.

"It's too late for that. If you want to die here, I won't stop you," Sae said before kicking her horse into motion, riding it out of the stable and into the pouring rain. Quinn ran after her but tripped in the mud and fell onto his hands and knees with a splash. He looked up as Sae and her horse's figure disappeared into the heavy rainstorm as they galloped down Parika' Te Mo's only road out.

Quinn cried out to her in anguish, but the downpour covered the noise. There, almost drowning in the mud, he could only condemn his own foolishness. For he had, in a moment of anger and frustration, said both too much and too little at the same time. Later on, though, after the time of this account, he would come to loathe himself for those words for an entirely different reason.

For that was the last time he ever saw her. The red-haired woman, the realist Rogue Caster he had grown to care for deeply over the four months they knew each other. You see, it is then and there that she disappeared from written and oral history as quickly as she came into it, with Quinn the last to see her alive.

What happened to Sae? Did she escape the noose that was enclosing Parika' Te Mo's township and people? Let's just say she did. And that the search party that was sent after her once the Serpents had left for the Deep Woods and the storm had cleared was wrong in their assumptions when they found her horse, dead along the road.

Chapter 4 – Bravado

Always retain the respectfulness of a gentleman. Refrain from rude language and crude conduct.
—Fourth Oath of the Silver Serpents

It seems that now is as good a time as any to do a decent introduction of the various members of the Silver Serpent Akuan, our story's heroes. The brave men who dared to trek into the dangerous, unforgiving swamps beyond Parika' Te Mo and then on into the Void, spawn–infested Deep Woods, the most dangerous hidden corner of all Danneish.

While all Danneishie know most of the well-known Silver Serpent stories by heart by now, perhaps are even able to speak each of its members' names from memory, that might not be said for the rest of the world. Rather than write lengthy biographies and descriptions of the lads I had many occasions to personally meet, I shall instead do the more "fun" thing.

I shall tell you what they joked about, what they sang about, what they argued about. For that, I believe, is the best biography one can write of another, as these things act as windows into the soul of a human being. Something that a comparatively lengthy biography without feeling would never do justice.

***

It was the day after, when the rainstorm cleared, and the Silver Serpents, eager to hunt their new prey, ventured through the swamps on foot. Through terrain and bogs so horrid that the smell could almost petrify a man. Or so Tryan kept saying. A keen sense of smell that one had.

Yes, with packs on their backs and a child's coffin between Bryon and Quinn's shoulders, they toiled relentlessly forward as the swampland east of Hooken Hills acted like the monster the locals knew it to be. It tried and tried again to suck the Serpents into it with its mud and muck. It attacked them viciously in the form of swamp snakes, large alligators, and even Void-afflicted insects that grew to be the size of bears.

Not to mention the more insidious ways that the hazardous landscape tried to attack our fair heroes. For example, the unending swarm of mosquitos, which would drive you mad from bites and itching and later could kill you with malaria.

Regardless of these perils, the Silver Serpents continued onward in good order. They held the bravado of men afflicted not by the all-consuming monster that was the swamplands, but by the cheer of those embarking on a pleasant walk through a flower-laden meadow on a midsummer's day.

You see, for Akuansmen, for human-shaped blades as tough as these men, dangerous terrain was no inconvenience, just par for the course of their life's roadless journey. So they spoke casually together as they walked toward the epicenter of the incoming tragedy.

"So, which one of us won the bet then?" said Red as he looked at Quinn out of the corner of his eye with a smirk. Red, the former thief, was always very cheeky. Quinn, sensing what he was about to be in for, said nothing. He just focused on not letting his boots get sucked in and lost in the muddy water beneath him, hoping to whatever God exists that he would not accidentally step on anything that could bite him in the waist-high swamp water they were all cautiously wading through.

"Wasn't it you, Seppa? Didn't you bet that they'd last between four and five months?" said Bryon as he labored with Quinn to keep the child's coffin, which weighed over nine stone, above the swamp water.

"I wish. I said two months, remember? Samson, wasn't it you who said just over four months?" Seppa replied while pulling the roots of a mangrove tree aside, helping Bryon and Quinn to get past a tight gap between two root-riddled swamp trees.

"No, I didn't take any part in this bet," said Samson as he and Fredstar helped the ailing Tar through the murky, swampy waters. The fact that a man in his seventies was able to navigate that difficult terrain with only a little help and without slowing down the party was an impressive feat not lost on anyone.

"Bells, if it wasn't you, then who won the bet? There are over fifty glints in the pot. That's enough for five men to get well hammered twice over," said Bryon in distress, obviously thinking he would be one of those five men once the winner was named.

"It was Michael. He won the bet," Tar said, answering the question as the swamp water started to go up to their chests.

"Michael, it was you? Why'd you not say anything?" said Bryon, looking over his shoulder at the recluse named Michael.

"Because I wish I hadn't made that bet in the first place. It's not right to bet against your own failing. I realize that now. This is supposed to be a brotherhood, after all," the man with the scarred face said with a hint of regret.

"Ya ova thinkin' it man. Just take our money and buy us all a round of drinks. Quinn won't bloody care, will ya lad? It's not like they were married or anything," said Gus as Quinn quietly endured the conversation. "I mean, at least she gave you somethin' to remember her by. A big slap on the face, as red as the sun it was."

The Serpents couldn't help but laugh at the memory of seeing Quinn return alone to the graveyard in the pouring rain, covered in mud with Sae's bright-red handprint on his cheek. He had said with deadly seriousness (as was his usual way of speaking) three simple words: "She is gone."

The men laughed as Tryan quoted Quinn's words on that day. They found heavy use for that quote the following morning. And they used it on every opportunity they could. When the morning campfire went out, Lichale reported that she was gone.

41

When Seppa frightened a pair of alligators away from their group, he said that she was gone twice.

Even Tar got in on the action to make fun of Quinn's embarrassing parting of ways when he told them all that the part of the swamp they were trekking through had no name. And so he decided to name it *Hanjigo mer so'fet degi*. Translated from the ancient Petascript, it loosely means, "the Swamp of woman who unceremoniously went away."

For Quinn, the bottom rung of the Silver Serpent totem pole, the man with the face of a noble king yet no kingdom, their mocking simply meant he was fitting in. For these were the kind of men who would only make fun of people they liked and would never share jokes with a perceived enemy. Quinn, having seen this kind of mockery between the Serpents before, knew that it was simply his turn to endure it. It would soon blow over, so he held his tongue. Mostly.

"So, Quinn. Although we all knew it was gonna happen eventually, how'd ya do it? How'd you screw things up with our little sister?" said Lichale as he caught a swamp snake swimming across the water in front of him with his bare hand. He then chopped off its head with the dagger kept on his shoulder. Then he threw it over his back, thinking it would make a good addition to their lunch later.

"I don't want to talk about it," Quinn said in a monotone, eyes forward.

"That bad, huh?" said Tryan as he shook his head with fake seriousness, trying to be funny.

"Mate, if things were going south with her, you should have come to me. I know everything there is to know about women, twice over in fact," said Gus, one of the most obnoxious men you'd ever meet, prone to foot-in-mouth syndrome.

"Gus! Giving courting advice ... Boys, I can't believe I'm saying it, but we are reaching levels of irony here I previously thought impossible," said Tryan with a whimsical smile.

"Shut your face Tryan, you bloody nitwit. Been with more girls than you ever have."

"Ah yes, and I just wonder how many of that large number discretely slipped you the bill afterward," Tryan replied, to which everyone, even Quinn, laughed. That was, except for the now-slighted Gus and the humorless former Sergeant Fredstar.

"Enough, lads. Remember the Fourth Oath," said Fredstar, trying to curtail this conversation into something more becoming of proper gentlemanly conduct.

"Don't worry Quinn. She'll forgive ya eventually. The good sorts always do," said Michael, still feeling a touch bad for his probationary Silver Serpent brother.

"Quinny. I told you from the start that Sae would only be trouble. You should have never tried to court her. An Akuansman's wife is the open road, and my, is she a jealous lover," said Tar with authority in his tone, wishing to use this example of heartbreak as a lesson for his men against hangers-on.

It was quiet for a while before Bryon, unable to read the now somber mood, said, "How do you feel about all this, Quinn? Are you really upset or somethin'?"

Quinn grabbed Red and led him to swap places with him holding up the child's coffin before saying in a pissed-off tone, "Excuse me while I go drown myself in that bog over there."

***

It was not long after Quinn decided against using suicide to escape his great embarrassment that the Serpents, still up to their chests in swamp water that concealed many dangerous horrors, all decided to sing some cadence to keep morale high.

Actually, it was not so much a group decision but more Fredstar, the second adjunct's command, that compelled them all to do so. He thought a good round of cadence was the elixir of life for a soldier's soul. Nobody had the heart to tell him, the career military man in another life, that while most Akuansmen act like soldiers, they certainly aren't.

Yet Tar and First Adjunct Samson allowed the command, as the order and conduct of the Silver Serpents was Fredstar's main responsibility. They dared not infringe upon his area of authority. The lesser Serpents, however, always found ways to mess with their by-the-book former sergeant and often did so with great pleasure.

"We gonna kill," sung Fredstar.

"KILL," sung all the Serpents.

"We gonna slay."

"SLAY."

"We gonna make pay."

"PAY."

"So is our way."

"So is our way," the Serpents echoed.

"No Marhin Jike is gonna mess with us."

"Nay nay nay."

"No Berthan Knight is gonna behead us."

"Nay nay nay."

"No Kijon De'sus is gonna ruin us."

"Nay nay nay."

"Nay, nobody is tough enough for us."

"Nay nay nay."

As the cadence continued over the sound of slushing swamp water and Tryan almost falling over when his boot got stuck on an unseen root, Gus stopped singing and leaned over to complain to Quinn quietly.

"Here I am, up to my tits in foul swamp water, and I've got to sing about how fakkin' tough we are. I have to say, I'd feel much tougher without wet tits."

Quinn smirked at Gus's remark as he watched the man smile to himself.

Lichale, overhearing Gus's candid remark, came beside Quinn and Gus, then said quietly, pretending to talk only to himself, "What you up to, Lichale? Oh, nothing much, I'm just marching to the Deep Woods, hell incarnate. Do I want to sing some cadence on the way there? NO. I don't want to sing some fakkin' cadence. I want to shit myself and run away."

The men who heard, which was most of them, stopped singing to Fredstar's tune and started laughing instead, causing Fredstar to stop his marching tune entirely.

"What are you lads yammering about? I can't hear your voices. Tryan, are you being a nuisance again?" Fredstar said from the front of the Silver Serpent procession.

"Not this time, sir," Tryan said honestly.

"I don't believe you. If you don't think that this cadence is entertaining enough for you, how about you lead us in one that you think is?" said Fredstar, dressing the man down a little.

"Fair enough sir. I think I know just the tune to lift one's step," Tryan said as he grinned from ear to ear behind the backs of the three senior Akuan members and looked at his brothers.

"Have you heard the one about the valley far yonder, sir?" Tryan asked, to which all the Serpents who knew the song started to smirk.

"No. I don't believe I know that one. Proceed," said Fredstar, not knowing what he was in for.

"Come on lads. Let's sing this loud and proud, shall we?" said Tryan with a devilish grin.

"Come on then, sing us up one of your roguish ballads to halt our mouths from all this complaining," added First Adjunct Samson.

Tryan dramatically cleared his throat as they continued through the swamp, which seemed to be getting more and more shallow by the moment. The branches of the mangroves overhead too started to become less dense, revealing blue sky above for the first time in hours.

"In a valley not far from here lies a town of which I hold dear," Tryan sung, with quite a nice voice, I must add.

"Bells, this bloody song again," said Seppa under his breath as Tryan continued.

"Its name upon my heart I call upon when I seek its tender relief. But when I travel there, I am only met with constant grief."

"Ffffoooorrrr!" The rest of the men joined in, excluding Seppa, Fredstar, Samson, and Tar.

"All the men of Askusa, all the men hate me. All the men of Askusa, all the men hate me."

"Why do they hate ya, boy?!" Gus cried out.

"Cause I slept with their daughters, I slept with their wives. While they were busy ploughing their fields, I was ploughing their—"

"ENOUGH! I don't think we need to hear the rest of that song, do we?" a stern, red-faced Fredstar said to the men who had been singing.

"It violates the Fourth Akuan Oath, idiots," said Seppa, who sometimes acted like he was too good for life's simple pleasures.

"Come on Fredstar. We are in the middle of bloody nowhere. Whose gonna hear our cussing out here?" Tryan pleaded.

"Yeah, my brother's right. I don't think the swamp lizards care too much what we say," said the dumb giant called Bryon.

To which Quinn felt the need to add, "They are called alligators, Bryon. Alligators."

***

After the indelicate happening, which Tryan later called a good "piss up," it was decided that the lesser Serpents could not be trusted to sing what was proper, meaning there'd be no further cadence that day. Much to the relief of everyone present except Fredstar.

That bout of good news coincided with the Serpents finally making it through the worst part of the swamps, meaning they were now only up to their ankles in mud and muck, improving the quality of their trek dramatically.

The Serpents were now heading, you see, through the place called the Reed Sea, in which reeds of various types grew out of shallow, muddy water for fathoms in each direction. All as tall as a Broohina giant, they towered over the men at nine feet.

That, coupled with the fact that no trees grew overhead there, meant it was almost impossible to navigate through the reeds in a straight line once within. That was, unless one paid careful attention to the positioning of the sun and time of day to then derive the direction of north.

This was something all the men were very well versed in. And so, like the other natural obstacles encountered by the Serpents those first few days of the trek toward the Deep Woods, they met the challenge with little difficulty, continuing their stroll into damnation with high yet cautious spirits.

"The fact that we have men as old as seventy in this Akuan proves how good we are. If you can survive into old age in this profession, it means you are the best of the best. In fact, if you ever see an Akuan where all the lads and ladies are in their twenties, it means it's shite. They are probably all fresh recruits, replacements for the ones who got recently killed. I reckon anyone with any skill as an Akuansman would need to survive to at least middle age in an Akuan to be proven good," said Michael, sharing his theory on Akuanship with them all as they walked.

"Is this your backward way of saying I'm shit at my job, Mike?" said Tryan in good humor.

"Not only is he saying that, he's also saying that he's shit as well. You both are in your twenties. Heck, Quinn, Bryon, Michael, Seppa. You lot are too," said Gus, picking Michael's theory apart with a grin.

"I didn't mean it like that," Michael said seriously.

"We know what you meant, laddie. I agree, fresh recruits are always the ones to get killed first. Better not to have any at all. Isn't that right, Quinn?" said Tar with a smile.

"Yes, sir," Quinn replied as he followed in the footsteps of Seppa, who was hacking his way through the wall of green reeds with a hatchet brought for this very purpose.

"Yeah, hurry up and become a full member, Quinn. I'm sick of introducing you as the new guy when we meet other Akuans," said Lichale, who now carried the child's coffin with Tryan as it was their turn.

"I'll try my best," said Quinn, still in a bad mood from before. It was only one more month before his fate within the Akuan would be decided.

It was then, while they trekked single file through the Sea of Reeds, that a great animalistic shrieking call went out throughout the swamplands. Echoing from seemingly all directions at once, its unexpected and unwelcome arrival had all the Serpents freeze in place as they waited cautiously for any accompanying movements. But disconcertingly, none ever came.

"What the bells was that?" said Seppa, the point man and thus the most vulnerable of the procession.

"It sounded like a bird. A very big one," added Samson.

"A Fritgetay? Or perhaps a Mollowgrover or Bunziopion?" said Red, his tone matching the rest of the group's sudden seriousness.

"Fritgetay don't have mouths they can squawk like that with, remember," Michael said as he unslung his bow.

"There's no large, bird-like Voidlings in these parts. Its call must be bigger than its bite," theorized Fredstar.

"Easy, laddies. We aren't no third-rate Akuan as Michael was saying just a minute ago. We don't get scared from hearing the cry of a Voidling we have never heard before. We aren't no freshies, are we?" Commander Tar said as the voice of reason.

His men nodded, and the Serpents, now pondering whatever horror had made the bloodcurdling call, trekked onward through the reeds with fresh seriousness. For the first time since entering the swamps, a real danger had presented itself.

"Never heard anything like that before. Not even a Two Tail's scream is as haunting," Red said as he kept careful watch on the blue sky overhead.

"Ya think it's the rainbow bird from Pell's story?" asked Bryon, somewhat worried.

"That story said it had no head. How does it make a warning cry like that without a mouth?" said Michael, who now had an arrow out, ready to be fired. Seppa, the Akuan's designated marksman, ordered Quinn to switch with him hacking at the front so he could draw his bow. An attack could come from anywhere at any time, they thought. Tar, however, thought otherwise.

"Relax, relax. If it's really coming to kill us, we'll hear it long before we see it. Something that big-sounding can't be totally silent like us. What's with you lads today? You usually have more heart than this," Tar said as he walked in the center of the procession between his two adjuncts.

"I guess our growing proximity to the Deep Woods has everyone on edge, sir," said Samson, naming the likely culprit.

"Yeah, it's not far now, lads, until we meet our doom," Tryan said as a kind of half joke as he repositioned the heavy coffin on his shoulder.

"You joke about it, but the reality of where we are going is starting to set in," Seppa said, still watching the sky. It was at this moment that Red got his boot stuck and fell over into the mud because he was paying more attention to what could have been above rather than what was in front of him.

"Shit! Days like today have me questioning why I ever put my hand up for the Akuan life," Red said as he sat in the swamp water, wiping mud off himself.

"It was to escape the hangman's noose as I recall," Samson said.

"I did nothing wrong. I wasn't a thief; I was a courier for people who didn't know they wanted their goods delivered to someone else. It was all just a series of misunderstandings really," said Red with a cheeky smirk.

"Is that why you keep stealing my socks? Because you think I don't want them anymore?" asked Lichale.

"Once a thief, forever a thief. You haven't changed a bit, have ya, Red?" said Gus as he helped the red-haired man up to his feet. He then continued with the procession as Quinn kept forging a path forward.

"Let me remind you, Red, that not only did you join an Akuan to escape death, just as Michael did to escape slavery and Seppa his gambling debts, but you also took up the Akuan mantle to get something in this world that cannot be obtained any other way," Tar said before pausing for a moment while he ordered Gus and Lichale to take up possession of the coffin with a quick hand movement.

"That being freedom, sir?" Quinn asked as he continued hacking away at the swamp reeds.

"Precisely. In this world exist those who work for others and those who work for themselves. We do both simultaneously. As men who are above the law of kings, only accountable to our Oaths and our Akuan brethren, we are lucky to live with total autonomy.

"While most common folk live lives of serfdom under their local lord, we make our own way, our own roads. We all joined an Akuan to escape our previous existences, trapped in the mundane perpetual grind of everyday, for we knew no freedom there. Hear me, laddies, hear me well. I'd rather be slain by a Voidling as a freeman upon this great endeavor than die from old age as a nameless subject."

"Aye aye," said all the Serpents, agreeing with the notion presented by Tar with his effortless confidence.

"It's funny, Red. The more I hear Tar talk, the more I trust him. The more I hear you talk, the less I trust you," said Tryan, the Akuan's jokester, to which his brothers laughed.

"Sir, I've found something," Quinn said, interrupting them as all eyes focused on him. Quinn, with help from Seppa, parted a group of reeds to reveal the two-day-old, decomposing remains of a human body in swamp water. The Serpents gathered around as they examined it closely in silence. When they saw the manner in which this man died (made visible from the large claw marks across the body's chest), they realized the truth.

Any one of them could end up just like this Danneishie Ranger, just like so many fresh Akuan recruits too. Any one of them could be the one to get killed next. For it is one thing to say you wish to die free, another entirely to actually do it.

"It dropped him . . . whatever it was," Fredstar said despondently.

"He didn't even get time to bleed out from the claw wounds. The brains leaking out from his skull show that he died on impact with the ground," said Samson.

"To pick up a fully grown man and drop him from high enough to break his face like that . . . The Voidling must be huge," Lichale added.

"It's strange it didn't eat him. The bite marks are just from passing animals," Quinn said.

"Maybe it didn't have a mouth to eat with," said Bryon, hearkening back to Pell's story. Nobody was pleased at that thought.

"Why is a lone Ranger out here anyway? I thought they only travelled in pairs and not around here anymore," said Michael.

"Perhaps he was taken from far away then dropped here," Red guessed.

"The local Rangers told Tar and me when we took this contract in the village head's house that we'd have a clean run all the way to the Deep Woods. No major Voidling threats. He assured us of that fact," said Fredstar.

"I've been assured? Sound like words to die horribly by," said Tryan with dark humor.

"Enough! All of you," Tar said seriously as he looked each of his Serpents in the eye. "I know what you are all thinking but won't say aloud. That you don't want any part of this. Each of you have already decided that this is a foolish, suicidal mission that we could have kept well away from. It's why complaining has been included in so much of your bravado on the way here; I understand now.

"But understand this, as this dead man before us must have understood before he fell, the time for joking, for complaining, is now over. Regardless of your uneasy feelings on the subject, we are going to do this. We shall slay the Forbidden One, whatever the cost."

Tar looked over his men. He didn't want to describe this mission like this before because he didn't wish to scare anyone, but now he realized he had to. He needed to direct their natural fear of the Void into obedience to his command. To an Akuansman, a commander's word must be absolute. While Akuans like to say they have no kings or queens, each grouping serves at the pleasure of their self-elected commander.

Seeing Tar's resoluteness in his dark, piercing eyes, each man finally gave up hope on turning back early. This mangled corpse of the Forest Ranger before them confirmed at least one aspect of Pell's tall tale. A new Voidling had indeed taken up residence in the Deep Woods, one which the common folk, the Danneishie Rangers, and even the Lore Masters knew almost nothing about.

Chapter 5 – Alien Hands

What is the Void? The question that has plagued humanity since its infancy. Even our ancient human forebearers the Oath-Keepers, whose long-lost technology and insights are the subject of exhaustive studies the world over, even they claimed themselves ignorant on this subject.

So instead of a scientific answer, I can only give hypotheses and theory. The Void and its growing presence on our world are our destruction, some have said. Others have said it is simply the natural chaos of the greater universe correcting the singular oddness brought upon by our dimension's laws of physics, which, to our knowledge, are not repeated anywhere else.

Perhaps it is as the poets and religious folk have described, the natural manifestation of evil, of hate in this world. That when the sins of a great number of people gather in one area, an otherworldly tear will open producing horrific Voidspawn in endless number, is a widely accepted cultural mythos spanning many different peoples.

Or perhaps none of the above. For while it is much talked about with many interpretations, I fear none truly know, and perhaps none will ever come to know in any of our lifetimes what the Void really is. Despite this, there is one truth we can all agree upon. When it comes to the strange, otherworldly presence called the Void, it is science, not magic, that governs its unwanted appearance.

For it has been said repeatedly by those wisest and most educated among us, by Gifted and Ungifted alike, that magic, much like the fabled unicorn or pixy, does not exist in this world but only in one's imagination.

Almost every educated person knows that Casters do not cast their supernatural Gifts through spells but through their corrupted biology exerting itself through parallel universes, which possess laws of physics that can supersede and twist those of our own universe. Thus, a man can produce fire from his hand and not be burnt by it.

The great Xenobiologists, the Lore Masters, and the Mathematicians, their star-hunting colleagues who track our world's rotation around the sun, all say science, not magic, governs our world called Terranova.

They further theorize that the Void and its corruption of the natural universe are likely the impact of another parallel universe's unwelcome presence on our own. In essence, they speculate that the Void is simply a visitor, an alien dimension mingling with our own.

I myself, a Bard who travels to many a place both as a welcome visitor and sometimes even an unwelcome one, often wonder what brought this suspected alien traveler to our door. Is the Void alive? Can it think? Or is it simply a habitat for alien beings, which burst from it in both animalistic and sentient forms?

As a poet, as a singer-songwriter, and a storyteller of growing regard, these unanswered questions are the focus of many of my thoughts as I sit here today in my warm office in peaceful downtown Tellicone. As the evening sea breeze gently caresses me through my open window while the curtains flutter, I am free to indulge in these high-minded ideas. Ideas enabled in this feudalistic fourteenth century by ancient Oath-Keeper texts, enlightenment from a dead civilization.

But such thoughts of intellectualism were not on the minds and hearts of the Silver Serpents that day when they first saw it. The first real challenge that the Forbidden One threw their way when they finally reached the Deep Woods. The corrupted forest of the Void.

The difference between what artists and intellectuals like me have said about what the Void is and what others, the ones who must actually deal with its spawn on an almost daily basis, have said is almost as stark a difference as night and day, wet and dry.

To a monster-hunting Akuansman like any of the Silver Serpents, the Void is both a livelihood and an eventual early grave. It is not something to be pondered or intimately understood but something to be overcome, outmaneuvered, then destroyed for coin.

The Void is your enemy. That is all you must understand, and that is all there is to know. And so those Void-weary Serpents went into the Deep Woods that day knowing that they'd need to kill everything they saw. And let me tell you, there was much to kill.

While variety may be the spice of life, in the Deep Woods, where many different types of Voidlings lurk, variety is the spice of one's death. But I'm getting ahead of myself. So I shall finish the introduction to this chapter with a thought not of my own. For it was Devyn Vernon, the Grand Bard of the Five Strings, who once beautifully said this of the Void when he was asked to describe it:

"Just as all good must come from somewhere in this world, all bad must come from somewhere as well."

***

A day later.

"Well, that's fakked up," said Gus as he and his Serpent brothers stood in disgusted awe before a mess of gray-skinned, decomposing bodies. Twenty in number, they lined the entrance to the Deep Woods with mangled forms and dried blood. By all appearances, they had been slaughtered as dusk fell while they set up camp.

Having left the Reed Sea behind them a day ago, the Silver Serpents had been trekking through the maze-like forested outskirts of the Deep Woods for a while. There not being any natural border to the place, they weren't initially sure until they found the massacred Logging Guild party, last seen over a month ago, that they had found the area where the Forbidden One was said to live.

"What the bells killed them?" said Quinn, turning over a corpse with his blade, looking for any cause of death.

"Look at this one here . . . the way the body is positioned. It's almost like he died screaming," said Red, examining another corpse set against an old oak with a great look of fear-induced concern on his face.

Michael, seeing that under one of the corpses was a weatherproof pouch of some kind, tried to lift the corpse with a nearby stick. However, the weatherworn flesh tore open, and out of it exploded a mess of small bug-like Void parasites, which had been living inside the corpse.

"We'd be better able to tell what killed these men if these bodies were still in one piece," Michael said, trying not to throw up at the sickening sight before him.

"Found their supplies. At least what is left of them," Lichale said, opening a sack of moldy flour, then one of rotten venison, and another with blue cheeses.

"Can't you eat blue cheese?" said a hungry Bryon as he and Gus looked into the third sack.

"I'd rather throw up into my mouth for food than eat that shite," said Gus as he walked away, to which Lichale dropped the sack with a smirk and then joined him.

"Remember, lads. Get a good look but don't take anything with you. It'll only slow us down. We packed light for a reason," said First Adjunct Samson as he looked over his men searching the camp of the dead Foresters.

"What about their coin?" said Red as he dangled a filled coin purse in front of him.

"The Voidlings will hear those silver glints in your pocket from a fathom away. Are you trying to get us killed?" said

Fredstar, prompting Red to, against his instinct, put back the bulging coin purse at the corpse where he found it.

"We have all we need to kill the Forbidden One, laddies. All we need," repeated Tar as he stood next to the child's coffin, his two adjuncts to his left and right overseeing the scene with him.

"Except arrows, sir. Brothers, take any that you see," said Seppa as he ripped an extra quiver from one of the Foresters' bodies. The monster that produced the great bird-like shriek heard a few days ago still weighing heavily on his mind.

"Sirs! You gonna wanna see this," said Tryan from beyond the half-set-up camp. The Akuansmen, eager to see whatever it might be, dropped what they were doing to come to where Tryan was, among old oaks and undergrowth. The forest there was so dense that it prevented one from seeing beyond forty feet.

Quinn and the others came to Tryan's side and all looked down upon the blue, blood-laden ground at the thing he had found. It was well-built and tall, a humanoid with blue skin and pristine white hair. It was covered from neck to toe in tribalistic tattoos, with the black horns of a ram coming from its head. It was a being from the New World. A Jike. It wore a loincloth as its only garment as it was a male.

"A Jike?! What's a Jike doing here?" said Michael, asking the question on everyone's mind.

"Looks like it died of natural causes for a Jike. Arrow poisoning," said Gus as he wiped his nose on his sleeve then spat.

"Where there is one Jike, there is usually many. Could there be a Jike mob nearby?" pondered Fredstar.

"Was he maybe the guide for the Foresters?" said Tryan, offering an opinion.

"A Jike guide would explain why they were able to make it all the way here in one piece," said Samson, entertaining the thought.

"Then why did he get an arrow in his heart if he was working with the human Foresters? Voidlings don't use bows," said Quinn, to which nobody had any answer. Except Tar, who seemed to have one as he crouched before the Jike corpse.

"See this, laddies?" Tar ran his open palm against the Jike's blue-skinned chest. "You aren't able to see it as clearly on the Forester's bodies because we humans decompose much faster than Jikes, but this Jike's skin is covered in handprints."

The Serpents crouched to see this for themselves. Samson lit a torch and put it over the body so they could see the Jike's blue-tattooed skin better in the darkness of the forest.

"By the Saints!" uttered Fredstar as all of them finally saw what Tar was talking about.

"Handprints ... there's at least a hundred of them," said Seppa, aghast in horror.

"Whatever he was doing here, it seems he died to whatever strangeness is befalling this forest. Hmmm, perhaps this Jike was indeed their guide. Perhaps this was a mercy killing," said Tar as he continued to look over the Jike's barely decomposed, fully intact body.

"Had this Jike not died from the arrow through the heart, whatever creature put its hands on him would have killed him like the Foresters he led. Hmm ... sounds plausible, sir," said Samson as he scratched his beard, finishing Tar's thought.

Everyone stood in silence around the corpse, thinking of the implications that line of logic would suggest, when Quinn said, "They're not the size of an adult's hand, perhaps a child's?" At his words, everyone made a terrible revelation on their own. The same one in fact.

Tar pulled away from the Jike corpse, ordering quickly, "Serpents at the ready!"

The Silver Serpents, fearing the worst, rushed back to the site of the massacred Foresters and then slowly approached what lay in the center of the camp. The very thing they had brought there to fight the Forbidden One. The child's coffin was now an unknown element. A potential threat.

With blades out and arrows drawn, the Serpents took up their favorite horseshoe formation around the target. Slowly and silently, they moved toward the coffin, which lay nailed shut. Nobody had checked its contents since the graveyard in Parika' Te Mo.

If a child was these dead Foresters' assailant, could it be theirs as well? the Serpents thought. However unlikely it was that something had taken possession of their child's corpse without them realizing it, they weren't going to take a chance. As nobody ever knows anything for certain when dealing with the Void.

Tar issued the order for the two point men, Quinn and Tryan, to carefully bust it open. One step. Two steps. They inched closer as Seppa and Michael pulled tension on their war bows. Quinn, unafraid of death, volunteered to be the one to crack open the coffin, mostly because he saw the fear in the eyes of Tryan across from him, prompting him to take the larger risk so his brother didn't have to.

Quinn took a careful knee beside the coffin and slid his seven-inch finishing blade under the nailed coffin lid. He waited a moment, then looked around at his nervous but at-the-ready brothers-in-arms. Could this be the battle they were waiting for? Could this be when they'd finally meet the being called the Forbidden One?

Tar gave Quinn the nod, and he popped the coffin lid open. And . . . nothing happened. Nothing at all. They were all shocked. They had feared, no, naturally assumed the worst, and yet the worst wasn't happening.

Quinn leaned in over the coffin, as did Tryan. They relaxed as they realized their fears were indeed for naught. Debbie's young daughter was still as dead as they found her, only smelling slightly worse. A collective relief fell over the Serpents as they realized that the child's corpse had not been possessed.

"Bells, would have been a lot easier if the Forbidden One decided to show up already," Red muttered, sheathing his blade.

"Do we even know if the Forbidden One killed these people? It could easily have been something else," said Seppa, lowering his bow.

"We'll likely have to kill the Forbidden One's current host before it takes possession of another," said Tar as he gestured for Quinn to hammer the coffin lid back on. "Come on then, laddies. Nothing more to learn nor gain from stickin' round here. Onward."

Tryan then said with great annoyance as he threw up his hands in a questioning way, "Wait a second, you mean we'll have to kill it twice?!"

***

"Mate, can't you just enjoy being wrong about something for a change?" said Lichale as the Serpents cautiously moved through the twisted, dark forest. Sprawling, low-hanging vines, fallen trees, and undergrowth so thick that it made the Swamp of Woman Who Unceremoniously Went Away look like an open, paved road in comparison.

"I'm not wrong, am I? No Voidling I've ever seen has come close. How is Gus's sister not the ugliest thing alive?" said Red with a smile, trying to keep nervousness off his face.

"Shut ya mouths before I shut them for ya," said Gus, mostly out of habit, lacking any enthusiasm behind the threat.

"What do you think, Quinn? You saw Gus's sister as well that day," asked Bryon, trying to use this pointless conversation to keep his mind off the fact they were marching into hell. To their knowledge, nobody had ever trekked this far into the Deep Woods before, or at least no one who was ever seen alive again. Everyone was on a knife's edge.

"Everyone is ugly to someone's reckoning," Quinn said, not having any time for what was to him a stupid line of inquiry.

"Ha. That's a nonanswer if I have ever heard one," said Tryan as he helped pull Quinn up and over a large fallen tree trunk at the front of the group.

"Leave Gus alone. He doesn't need your shit. Especially today," said Michael from the other side of the tightly knit group. Now a ways into the Deep Woods, all eleven Serpents kept in visual contact with each other at all times. If you got separated from the group, you would likely never be found again. Not only was the Deep Woods difficult to navigate, but it was also filled with predators looking to take advantage of a lone Akuansman. There was safety in numbers, as everyone everywhere instinctively knows.

"I keep looking up at the treetops and seeing shadows of people. Tar, are you sure there are no Face-Stealers in these parts? I could have sworn I've seen them tracking us a dozen times now," said Seppa, looking up at the treetops far above them, continuing the nervous chatter but changing the topic. Quinn shuttered with anger upon the word *Face-Stealer* spoken aloud; he particularly hated that kind of Void-afflicted foe.

"Relax, there are no Face-Stealers around here. Voidlings like to hunt them the same as us," Commander Tar said, the only one in this party of monster hunters not perturbed by the dangerous place they were trekking through.

"I think that—"

Tar raised his closed fist, interrupting whatever Fredstar was about to say. Everyone halted. They set their ears to listen as they all ducked down into the forest's heavy undergrowth for concealment. Gus and Red gently put down the child's coffin.

They all had heard something. Worse still, it was the cry of something unknown. Like with many Voidlings, you usually hear it before you see it, and whatever this was, it was no exception to that rule.

"That's no Voidling. Is it just me, or is that somebody crying?" Tryan said quietly to Quinn, who had ducked beside him. After listening to the strange sound for a while, Quinn nodded, not understanding how it was possible to find someone this far into the Deep Woods but still agreeing, nonetheless.

Using silent Akuan hand signs, Tar started making orders to the rest of his Akuan through the underbrush. Tryan and Quinn looked back at him to see him sign these words in sequence: *two, point man, investigate, behind, tree, others, spread, ambush.*

Understanding immediately, the Serpents silently enacted the plan with no further direction given. Each man knew exactly what their role was. They had done this many times before. The Silver Serpents had found and slain many Voidlings during their trek through that infested forest by this point. Could this finally be the one they were seeking? They all excitably and fearfully pondered.

Tryan and Quinn moved up with caution and their blades out. As the designated point men for this campaign against the Forbidden One, they were bait for whatever this was. They walked slowly, keeping low and in cover. Carefully, they moved aside the vines that dangled overhead and avoided stepping on branches, choosing wet leaf litter instead. Like the snakes they were, they silently slithered closer and closer to their prey as its cries grew louder, more mysteriously human by the moment.

The two point men came to a large red stoa oak tree trunk blocking their target from view. They looked at each other for a moment, knowing that they were about to proceed past the point of no return. Neither man proving to be a coward in that stressful moment, Quinn went around the right base of the tree while Tryan went left.

Matching pace with each other, they came around the large tree trunk at the same time. There they saw what produced such noise and were instantly horrified. It was human, its hands tucked into its chest, and it was crying. Both knees on the ground, it faced the tree trunk. It was a child! Seemingly a young boy.

Tryan and Quinn stood there in shock for a moment, processing the fact that whatever being took this child's form could kill them in a way they still didn't understand, as it likely had with the Foresters. Was this the Forbidden One that they were seeking? In that moment, they didn't know.

As they recovered from their moment of shock and went to retreat as planned, the "child" suddenly stopped its crying. It snapped its neck around at Quinn, and with black eyes and a pale, otherworldly smile, said, "Hello . . . Quinn."

Quinn stabbed his short sword through the child's head without hesitation, defying Tar's orders. He stepped back as he ripped his sword from its head, revealing a gaping hole where it had been. The gory wound dripped black blood, which spilled all over the ground like sticky ink.

Quinn was stunned, as was Tryan, as the child, having effectively just been lobotomized by Quinn's blade, stood up undaunted. Laughing even. At the sight of this alien supernatural horror, Tryan ran, closely followed by Quinn. They retreated to the ambush point not far away, breaking their line of sight on the creature out of necessity. Something you should never do when fighting a Voidling.

Their brothers still in hiding, the duo stood back-to-back next to the coffin, blades readied for the alien creature to follow. And follow them it did. The waist-high underbrush in the direction they came from parted quickly as the child raced toward them. Scuttling at them with great speed, the alien parted the tops of bushes and long weeds as it traversed yards of forest floor in less than a second.

Guessing that his battle brother was not strong enough to take on the monster's charge, Quinn pushed Tryan aside and raised his blade in their defense as the "child," with the locomotion of a four-legged beast, sprung up out of total concealment in the underbrush and at them both.

Bent in ways that the human body should not allow, it came at them with a wide-open, fanged mouth and a forked tongue as long as a man's forearm. Quinn braced and took on the fiend, battling it back with his bloodied blade across the corners of the creature's jaw.

Quinn secretly activated his Caster mutation, which in this instance functioned like adrenaline. He diverted this power toward his quickly fatiguing muscles, preventing him from being knocked over by the force of the Voidling now thrashing at him, as it beat against his stomach with its small, shoeless feet. With hands covered in black soil from the forest floor, it beat at his shoulders and neck, leaving handprints galore.

Quinn struggled against it, releasing more supernatural power into his body so he could keep whatever had attacked him high and in the air, where it was an opportune target for his Akuan brothers.

Tryan, recovering from Quinn's push out of the way, came back at the creature Quinn was holding at bay with his blade. He lunged at the child's chest and connected, but in his panicked strike he missed his intended target, the monster's heart.

The deformed, sickening child then took two more hits in its back as Seppa and Michael loosed their arrows into it, having just come out of concealment with the rest of the Akuansmen. All but Tar, unable because of his lofty age, charged the child showing no fear, just determination and cold steel. This was it, they all thought. This was their ticket out of this nightmare forest forever.

The child, sensing this ambush was too much for it, used its still-human hands and feet to bounce itself off Quinn while it spat out his sword. Quinn was knocked onto his back by the sheer strength of the creature, which seemed to possess a martial power well beyond its weakly child's form.

"Thanks mate," Tryan said as he helped Quinn up, admitting to him in that moment that he could not have done what Quinn just did.

Losing the encirclement of their prey, Quinn and Tryan's Akuan brothers formed up in front of them with their blades out, all taking up defensive sword stances, except for Michael and Seppa, who preferred their bows over their blades. The Serpents watched in steadfast horror as the creature stuck like a lizard to a rock in its landing place upon the trunk of a tall stoa oak twenty yards in front of them.

The being, with a hole in its forehead, black eyes, and a long forked tongue that dripped foul green liquid, peered at the Serpents with an otherworldly grin. It had a hole through its stomach now, but it was not bleeding. Nor did it seem to care about the two arrows sticking out of its back. Through its fang-filled mouth, as its head cracked forward in a way that humans would consider broken, it said in a haunting, otherworldly voice, "If you believe in something, but it has no real effect on you, do you really believe it at all?"

The Serpents, not understanding what it was talking about, only that it was indeed sentient, spoke among themselves.

"This must be it lads," said a resolute Samson, squeezing the hilt of his blade.

"Is it dead or alive?" asked Seppa.

"From the looks of it, both," said Tar, who was now at the rear of the Serpents. He was the only one without a weapon out to ensure he was presented as a minimal threat. The last one that the being would likely come for.

"Didn't Pell's story mention a child like this?!" said Bryon, thinking aloud.

"Look at Quinn. He's covered in the handprints, the same as the Jike. It must be it! It must be the Forbidden One!" said Lichale as Red started to grind his teeth in stress.

"Silence! Attention to your enemy!" said Fredstar loudly as the being jumped from its perch on the tree trunk like a frog from a wall. Unexpectedly, it zoomed through the air, headed for Tar in the back of the party, but at the last second, Bryon brought his shield around and smacked down the fiend onto the leaf litter in a feat of pure brawn.

The Serpents then rushed it as soon as it fell on the ground. Stabbing it all over, they became madmen in that moment of pure bloodlust.

"Burn the child!" yelled Tar with rage. Gus stopped his stabbing to rush and take out his secret whiskey flask. He then took a final swig of his secret comfort drink before ripping the waterskin in two and covering the thrusting, deformed child at their feet in alcohol. Samson, having not joined in on the stabbing of the creature, threw his lit torch onto it, setting the fiend aflame.

The Serpents stood back as Seppa and Michael kept driving arrows into it again and again. The creature burned and lashed out with fury at those around it before finally slowing down and falling to the forest floor, dead.

Before anyone had time to react to the creature's demise, an orb of blue light lifted from the mangled child's body. In awe of this never-before-seen sight, the Serpents stood, trying to hide their eyes from its blinding light with their hands. Quinn, seeing that it was hovering in the air for too long and not fleeing into the corpse of the dead girl nearby, was the first to realize something was wrong.

"Why is it not going for the dead child?" he asked.

"I don't think it has the appetite for a dead host like we thought," uttered Fredstar.

"Run for your lives before it takes you!" Tar yelled.

But it was too late. In that next moment, the Body Snatcher, the Rellian, chose its unlucky victim. It burst into Fredstar's chest, knocking the second adjunct back into the air for ten yards before he tumbled to the ground. The Serpents recovered from the blinding light, then rushed over to Fredstar instinctively to help him.

"Stay back! Stay back!" ordered Tar, gesturing the same message with his hand, acting with a sense of desperation that his Akuansmen soon saw and then heeded. Their second adjunct then rose from the underbrush with a wide, otherworldly grin. Their hearts sank as they saw fully blackened, inhuman eyes upon the face of the man they had loved.

Quinn stood in shock; it had all happened so fast that there was no time to think. No one had considered the idea that it could take over living hosts as well as the dead. Was Fredstar now gone forever? The Forbidden One, having taken Fredstar's body, took a step forward and mouthed, "I am death—"

As if in slow motion, out of nowhere an arrow pierced Fredstar's chest, cutting off his sentence. It entered at the armpit, in a gap in the under armor they all wore, which allowed freedom of movement. Fredstar went limp and collapsed, the alien smile gone from his lips as quickly as it had come. He crashed to the forest floor with a thud. Unlike last time, no blinding blue orb came out of the corpse.

The Serpents looked to see where the arrow had come from, to see which one of them had made such a precise yet heartrending shot. They saw their brother Seppa lower his bow. Tears rolled down his cheeks for what he had done. He looked at them all with great guilt and sadness. He had the unwanted honor of ending Fredstar's twenty-eight-year career as an Akuansman.

As Seppa cried and fell to his knees in pain and Tar went to examine the body of his slain adjunct, the other men stood without a word. Fredstar, their beloved brother, was dead before them. They could not believe it. Nay, they didn't want to believe it. It had all happened so fast. Too fast for any man to process, and so, dumbstruck, they stood speechless for a long moment.

Then another realization came upon them. They had done it. They had killed the Forbidden One. They had slayed the beast they had come to slay, yet it made them pay a terrible, terrible price. A price that Seppa would carry for all of his days. The first casualty that the Silver Serpents suffered during their campaign against the Forbidden One was not killed by alien hands but by their own.

As the momentarily dumbstruck Akuansmen went to help console Seppa, Tar confirmed that the Body Snatcher was now forever dead. By piercing the corpse's heart yet again, this time with the pointed tip of his finishing blade, he made sure Fredstar would not turn undead.

Quinn, always the deep thinker, remembered a thought he once had as he watched the painful scene around him like a detached outside observer would. He thought about how, in this world, everything costs you something. A life for a life, as was seen with Sae, who jealously wanted him for herself and would have given everything of herself in return as payment.

A corpse for a corpse, as was seen with Telligood the Rogue Caster, who despite his words on the subject, ran away from home to hide in the swamps after murdering his sickly father. And finally, a Voidling for an Akuansman. The oldest and most frequent transaction in the book of life.

What is the Void? Quinn came to his own conclusion on that day. To him, the Void was nothing more than a mass grave for good men like Fredstar. A place where those who venture shall never return. The Void is death incarnate. A place of unfair trades.

Chapter 6 – The Next Step

Reward kindness with kindness. Reward spilled blood with more blood.
—Third Oath of the Silver Serpents

Three days later.

The Silver Serpents came to Parika' Te Mo in the lowest of spirits. They marched back from the Deep Woods not as the victors they would seem to be but as paupers, having lost a part of themselves that they could never reclaim. Fredstar, their second adjunct, their iron resolve incarnate and law unto himself on the proper conduct of an Akuansman, was now dead, buried, and gone. In that order.

When the silent, despondent Serpents came to the now desolate village of Parika' Te Mo, not one, not even one of them batted an eyelid or shed a tear for the tragedy before them, just as it had been with the tragedy behind them. They were overcome with an all-encompassing feeling that left them numb.

The Serpents trekked quietly along the village's main road, beset with collapsed houses, dead animals, and those who could not run away in time. The typical reinforced dwellings often called strong houses, which were common in remote villagers like this that had no all-encompassing wooden barricade, did not live up to their name in this case.

An iron door and double-thick log cabin walls were usually strong enough to keep out most lurking Voidlings during the night, but not this time. They were but a hindrance to whatever Void spawn had come for all the villagers. The Serpents avoided stepping on the corpses of the many black crows that littered the ground in the way a tree litters the ground with leaves in autumn.

The supernatural sight of thousands of crows seemingly struck dead by hitting an invisible wall high above brought

Lichale to his knees as he remembered seeing such a horrifying thing as a child growing up in east Orrian, near the Void-tainted lands there. It was clear to all a UVE had hit here, hard.

"The Void has gripped this place. Once it grips something, it never lets go," Lichale said in anguish as the Serpents inspected the scene of death around them. Not one thing was left standing. Not one thing left living. Thirty strong houses, thirty families. Over a hundred livestock between them. Chickens, cows, pigs, dogs, cats, absolutely everything was slain where it stood. Killed by an unseen force without a single mark on any of their bodies. Only a mysterious dripping of blood from their ears.

Everything they took up the contract for, the reason they sacrificed one of their number, was now dead, buried, and gone. Not in that order. Parika' Te Mo, nowhere incarnate, now stood as an open-air graveyard to all their hopes. The Forbidden One had made our heroes into fools who had waged a fruitless endeavor.

As Quinn watched his brothers cry on the inside at the sight around them, he remembered Sae's now prophetic words from when this village still had life in it. She had told him that Parika' Te Mo and its people were already doomed, that their destruction was assured. He had not believed her when she told him this, but he believed her now.

He had to; it was right in front of him. Quinn realized among the ruins of Parika' Te Mo that his initial dismissal of her was mostly because he didn't want to believe. He didn't want there to be a being, a Voidling, capable of doing such a terrible deed as this.

For if he had accepted her truth earlier, he would have had to accept the full extent of the Forbidden One's power over life and death, and like all his brothers-in-arms except Tar, he didn't want to. Humans do not want to believe there are things in this life that are more powerful than them. Quinn made this deadly mistake, as do many still.

Parika' Te Mo was cursed by the Forbidden One, a single alien entity more powerful than any they had known before, and it wasn't until the Serpents saw Parika' Te Mo destroyed that they admitted to themselves that it was so. Perhaps the most bitter realization made that day was when Michael, the Akuan's surgeon, reported that the village and its people had been destroyed only a day ago, according to the state of rigor mortis seen upon the villagers' bodies.

Meaning that the Rellian, the Body Snatcher that had taken Fredstar's and the child's bodies, was not the Voidling they were looking for. The Forbidden One, humanity's nemesis, was still out there, at large, and with its true nature still unknown.

***

With few words spoken between them, the Akuan made a fire and camped for lunch on the other side of the graveyard. They kept away from the village so as to try and distance themselves from the smell of death. A smell now so strong in the air that not even the noxious fumes brought on by the southernly wind from the swamps could provide any relief.

They sat there in despondence as the lowest of the low of mankind. On a log and tree stumps, as the fire cooked up a meal of swamp fish, they gathered what little strength grief had not yet taken from them.

Tar looked down at his boots while Lichale used an iron pot scavenged from the destroyed remains of the Pothole pub, which now really was just a pothole in the dirt, to cook fish stew. A dish that, because of its recent frequency on their menu, they were all very much sick of.

Samson, sensing the despair of his men, turned to Tar, who was lost in his own world as always, then said the first words heard in over an hour.

"What is our next step, sir?" At Samson's words, all eyes darted to Tar.

"Next step, huh?" Tar said, awakening from his deep thoughts. "It's simple really. Oath Three. The Forbidden One had one of its fiends kill our man. It shed our blood, and for that we must shed its blood also."

Tar's words did not go down well with his Void-weary men.

"But, sir . . . we know nothing of what we are fighting," said Michael.

"Fredstar wouldn't want us all to go on a suicide mission to avenge him. Bugger the Third Oath, I say. Otherwise, there won't be an Akuan left to follow it anymore," said Red with ill humor.

The rest of the Serpents didn't say anything to Red's unakuansmenlike suggestion. Under normal circumstances, you could get dishonorably discharged for the mere mention of Oath breaking. However, out of fear, each man was unduly tempted by the thought. As cowardice sells itself to all men equally, even those considered brave.

Tar looked over his men with a straight face. All eyes except Quinn's stared back at him. Each man telling him through their stares what they really wanted. That being to run. To flee the swamp and its unknown, otherworldly denizen. He then peered at the man next to him, his second-in-command, his trusted right hand. He was saddened to see the same look in Samson's eyes as well.

"The signatories of the contract are all dead. Even if we complete it now, we'd get no payment. Sir, with all due respect, there'd be no dishonor if we simply walked away," Samson said, a heavy sense of regret in his tone. Seeing the lack of resolve each full member of his Akuan had, Tar looked at the fresh recruit called Quinn.

"What say you, Quinny? Shall we retreat? Shall we run and become cowards in the face of the Void? In the face of humanity's enemies?"

"Quinn doesn't get a say, sir; he's still on probation," said Gus upon seeing that Quinn, unlike the rest of them, still had fight in him. In fact, upon hearing Tar's words, Quinn's eyes started to blaze. Quinn, the Nameless Man, has always had the battle rage in him, you see. He was livid at the thought of running away and making this someone else's problem.

"Isn't he risking everything of himself, as we all are, just by being here? I would think his life is worth a single vote in this unofficial tally of where we all stand, right?" Tar said, his eyes landing on Gus. Gus looked down; he could not argue against that fact.

"Tell us what you think, Quinny," Tar ordered, already knowing what Quinn was going to say by virtue of being the mind reader he always seemed to be. Quinn glanced across the firepit to Tar, his coconspirator within the Akuan.

Quinn knew Tar's most dangerous secret, one no other living man knew. This dangerous knowledge and the bond between Quinn and Tar that it created made Quinn Tar's unofficial, unannounced third officer. Now that Fredstar was gone, Tar would be relying on him even more, Quinn realized.

"It is not what I think but what Fredstar thought that is important. What did he always tell us? Fighting off death but one more day is the key to the human spirit," Quinn finally said.

"This is not the same," Tryan quickly cut in.

"Oh, really, it isn't? Last week I was a probationary member of the Silver Serpents, an Akuan so skilled and renowned that people in nearby countries sought you out to rid themselves of Rogue Casters nobody else could handle. Last week I was being tutored and challenged by the very best Akuansmen in the Eighteen Kingdoms. By an Akuan that would go to the Deep Woods and back ten times over if it meant avenging but a single wound inflicted on one of its brothers. But now, in this week, I sit not with those men I have come to know and respect. I sit among cowards. I sit with men who have lost all hope in themselves."

Nobody dared to look at Quinn. He was still technically an outsider to the Akuan as he had not sworn Akuan oaths yet. The fact that a newbie was educating veterans on their oaths and duty shamed them greatly. However, it was still not enough to convince them off the path that fear had chosen for them.

"Quinny, you took the words out of my mouth." Tar looked at his second-in-command, then his men, most of whom he had raised, nurtured, and been a surrogate father for. "The only thing that has changed here in this past week is that you men have stopped believing in yourselves. You are all giants, yet the Forbidden One has you thinking you are but ants."

At Tar's wise words, the fire behind Samson's eyes reignited. He realized he had it wrong, and it showed on his face. The others, however, were not so swayed.

"How many contracts have we taken? How many dangerous jobs have we done where nobody got so much as a scratch?" Tryan pondered aloud.

"It must be hundreds," Lichale added.

"Perhaps even a thousand by now," Bryon guessed incorrectly.

"But now . . . Fredstar's gone. Our lucky streak is over. By the Saints, it really happened. The toughest man in our Akuan is dead. Sir, that's what's changed. Not us," Tryan said, finally finishing his thought. After nobody said anything for a while, Tryan found himself saying, "I still feel terrible, absolutely awful that we had to bury him in those cursed woods next to two dead children."

"Bells, we are going to be working into the night to bury all the villagers," commented Michael, once again smelling death on the air.

Quinn and Tar looked at each other. They could both see now that the men were spiraling into a perpetual cycle of despair with their hopeless words and thoughts. Tar gave Quinn a nod to speak something kept hidden from them all until now. A crucial piece of information that Quinn had shared with Tar shortly after hearing it.

Quinn unceremoniously announced, "Sae was a Rogue Caster." Everyone turned to Quinn to see if what he had said was simply a bad joke. It certainly was not the time for messing around. However, the seriousness on Quinn's face told them it was not.

"Impossible. Sir, you'd know if—"

"I thought her a documented and lawful Caster, not a factionless rogue. That is all I shall say on the subject," said Tar, cutting Samson off. The Serpents reeled from the surprising revelation that their little sister, whom they had loved, was also their favorite prey, their despised enemy.

"Since fakkin' when?!" said Gus.

"Just what we need. More good news," said Seppa, now pissed off.

"She told me before we parted ways. Tar found out about it soon after. But that's not all," Quinn said with regretful seriousness.

"That's not all?! What are you gonna say next? She was the Forbidden One in disguise, wearing a bloody dress?" asked Gus angrily.

"She claimed to know something about the Forbidden One's true nature and what was happening in Parika' Te Mo."

"And?" asked Samson.

"She didn't reveal much to me, but she did make one thing clear. That as of six days ago, a noose had closed around Parika' Te Mo and the local area. Meaning the opportunity to escape from the curse brought upon by the Forbidden One is long gone."

"You suggesting we are tra-trapped?" Lichale said, stumbling with his words. "We are trapped here between a massacred town and the Deep Woods until we can lift the curse? Until we slay the Forbidden One? Whatever the thing is?"

"Yes, that's what Sae believed, and now I believe it too," Quinn said softly, which all the Serpents, excluding Tar, were instantly distressed by. To them, their last hope of living through this mess had been taken from them.

"How did she know this?" said Red as he stood then paced nervously back and forth where the others were still seated.

"She wouldn't tell me before she left. She wanted me to leave with her immediately, she was so afraid of it. I refused inelegantly, and she left in a huff."

"Fakk me, I'm doomed because Quinn can't fakkin' talk to women properly. You should have sat her down and got her to tell ya everythin' lad!" Gus said in growing anger.

"Can we be sure she was speaking the truth? She's a Rogue Caster, after all," Seppa added.

"She said that the Forbidden One wasn't a Body Snatcher like Tar had assumed, which turned out to be correct. If she was right about that, she was probably right about everything else," Quinn admitted, after which all eyes went to Tar, the Voidling expert.

"I saw the immense doubt in Sae's eyes when she first heard our plan at the graveyard. Please keep in mind that doubt was a two-way street between me and her. It wasn't that I didn't want to believe her, I just had no logical reason to take her opinion over mine. But now, upon seeing the destruction this Forbidden One can rend and going through the battle we had with the child, I realize that Sae was correct. There is a Voidling at work here none have ever seen."

"The question then is the same, sir. What is our next step?" Samson said, already thinking he knew the answer but wanting it said aloud for the sake of his men. Tar stood, his back clearly hurting him from all the difficult terrain the old man had traversed in recent days. His voice, carried by the southerly wind, held authority.

"Hope is only a strength when the situation is impossible. It is useless when the probability of success is high, for then you do not need to hope to believe. Hope is born as the silver lining of the darkness called despair. Hope, without impossibility to counter it, is as useless as good intentions." Tar smiled a brave grin before continuing.

"Sammy, Seppa, Gus, Red, Tryan, Bryon, Lichale, Mikey, and Quinny, our next step here today is to hope! We should all be glad that we have an opportunity, here and now in the bitter turmoil of our desperation and thoughts of what could have been, to practice a perfect hope! Bells, a fleeting hope that we can find and slay the Forbidden One is one of the few things we have left. Or have you lot all lost that too? All of you, I remind you here today that despite your outward appearance of situational cowardice, you haven't really changed. You are all still giants among men. Worthy of the Forbidden One's fear and the praise of every man, woman, and child we have been able to save in our lives."

At Tar's lofty words, each Serpent gave in. They gave into hope where before was only hopelessness. While this was the worst storm the Serpents had ever sailed through, Tar had steered them through all the others thus far. In the end, they could not bet on themselves, but they felt they could still bet on him.

The fish stew started to boil over, and Lichale quickly saw to it. Red finally stopped his nervous pacing, and the ever-curious Michael, seeing something out of the corner of his eye, went over to investigate while keeping within sight of camp.

"He's right, lads. Nothing's changed here. We are still in the shit," Tryan said half-jokingly, twisting the meaning of Tar's message for a quick laugh from his brothers.

"Tar's always right," said a hungry Bryon as he perked up upon realizing a good-smelling meal was in front of him.

"Except when Sae's right. Apparently, that supersedes everything," Quinn said as a throwaway comment that caused all his brothers to laugh brightly.

"Quinn courted a Rogue Caster. Tar was right again; he always says you have a terrible taste in women," said Seppa as the others laughed, having finally reclaimed their enthusiasm for life despite the death all around them. Quinn sighed deeply; his secret was out.

"I'm never going to live this down, am I?"

"Na mate. Never," Tryan said with a smile as the others laughed at Quinn's annoyance at the truth.

Tar, seeing that the battle for their minds had been won for now, even if the underlying damage was still there, turned around and noticed that Michael was headed toward the swampy shoreline.

"Come back here lad. Lunch is about to be served," Tar said to him, concerned.

"Just a moment, sir. Something strange is going on over here," Michael said as he came to the shore of the silent, inconspicuous swamp about fifty yards from their camp. Upon seeing Michael's seriousness, the Serpents stopped their laughing and casual banter to watch their brother as he stepped closer and closer to the swamp's edge.

"What are you lookin' at, Mikey?" asked Bryon loudly from their camp.

"Air bubbles are rising to the surface over here. A lot of them too. It's not normal," Michael said as he cautiously kept his approach.

"Get back from there lad! We still haven't sussed out this area yet," Samson ordered as Michael stopped in his tracks at the swamp's murky edge.

He turned his back on the swamp then relaxed, saying, "Yeah, so long as it isn't attacking us right now, it can probably wait until after lunch."

The Serpents watched in horror as behind Michael appeared yet another frightening revelation. The swamp water exploded in a fury, and from the muddy depths of the swamp came a spider as large as a house. Standing three times as tall as the six-foot Michael, it towered above him, posed to strike down upon him in a fleeting moment.

Michael, sensing something large behind him, turned to look up at the fiend, which Pell had described in his tall tale almost a week ago. The spider looked down at the small man in front of it, then grinned at him with a mouth filled not with fangs but with the teeth of a human, jawline and all. The monster, the alien, the fiend, the new Voidling before them, said these few words for all to hear: "Another taken, another lost . . . Yet another toy broken, of human cost."

#

The Serpents clambered up, readying their weapons, rushing forward toward their brother-in-arms, but it was too late. The Spider, drooling from the corner of its human-like mouth, snatched Michael and split him in two with its front teeth.

The Serpents were struck motionless, mouths agape at the sight of Michael's bloodied lower torso and legs falling into the murky water in front of where he previously stood whole.

Enraged at the sight of what they just saw, tempered with the feeling of injustice and being personally wronged, the Serpents came alive to their heroic selves in a mere moment. Tar, instead of speaking aloud his order, threw his fist up out of habit and commanded in Akuan hand sign language one word. Strangle.

Taking only their war gear, Seppa, Gus, Lichale and Red fled right of the swamp. Tar, Samson, and Bryon fled to the left.

Quinn and Tryan, still the two designated point men for this campaign, stood still at camp with their blades out. As the other men disappeared from the Voidling's sight, Quinn and Tryan stood defiantly as the bait.

The towering spider looked with its hundreds of eyes at the scene in front of it and judged it had the opportunity to move forward. It walked on six thick, hairy spider legs toward Quinn and Tryan like it had all the time in the world. Its leg tips sunk deep into the brown-green mud as it lumbered slowly along with drawn-out leg motions necessitated by its considerable weight.

"Quinn, don't do anything heroic like last time. If it comes for me, just let it. I should be the one protecting you as the recruit, not the other way around," Tryan said softly as the spider moved closer and closer to them with each lengthy step it took.

Quinn smiled, then said back, "Lose your pride, brother. You know I'm already better than you at this."

Tryan pushed Quinn aside gently with his shoulder to take up the position of lead bait, saying, "This isn't about pride. It's about making sure our best asset doesn't get eaten first."

Tryan smiled grimly back at Quinn before looking at the spider now picking up its pace toward them. Quinn gripped his sword hilt tighter as he knew what Tryan was about to do. He wished there was another way, but Tryan was right. A trade would have to be made, and it would be better for them all in this circumstance if it wasn't him.

The Toothy Spider, with great quickness in its stride, now lunged down at the nervous Tryan. Quinn, missing a swipe of its leg brought around in the charge, jumped upon the side of its now lowered head to hang onto its hairy body the best he could.

Meanwhile, as they had expected, the fiend's mouth opened to chomp down on Tryan. To counter this, the lead bait did the thing the toothy monster least expected. Tryan dived into the

Voidling's large human-like mouth without hesitation at the last moment, missing the spider's chomping teeth by a mere inch.

Quinn saw that Tryan had executed the first part of strangle, the ancient worst-case-only strategy, perfectly. He had successfully entered the Voidling while staying in one piece so he could now try to slay the creature from within. An act of insanity, some regular folk would say, but to a crazy Akuansman, it made perfect sense.

This dangerous bet that Tryan had made with his life hinged on the chance that he should be able to survive within the beast long enough to kill it from the inside. "Should" being the key word.

Quinn climbed up on the beast's head, behind the nexus of its many hundreds of red eyes. He did so in order to jam his sword into the fiend's exoskeleton there. After two quick unsuccessful stabs with his sword, he found he had to use the superhuman strength brought on by his Caster power to have any chance of penetrating it.

As Tryan started to slash inside the fiend's mouth, fighting for positioning against the being's human-like tongue, which fought to expel him, Quinn held on for dear life to his sword, which had pierced the very top of the spider's head. The spider thrashed side to side, hating the feeling of having something inside its mouth and on top of its head.

The rest of the Akuan came out in force from their concealed positions; it was now time for their part of the combined effort. With swords in hand, each man, even Tar, rushed toward each of the spider's six hairy legs. The seven men acted like Foresters and started to chop at the spider's legs whenever they touched the ground, which seemed like it wasn't often, as the spider was now turning in circles wildly.

The spider's senses were overwhelmed. The Serpents had executed the strangle strategy perfectly, even with their depleted number. Quinn found more Gift power within himself and slowly pushed his short sword deeper and deeper into the spider's head, knowing his blade was not long enough to risk hitting Tryan.

The Toothy Spider chomped and thrashed against them. In an act of desperation, it spun its legs around, trying to whack its human foes back.

"DUCK!" yelled Samson as he and Tar did so. However, Bryon, a larger target in stature and not as quick on his feet as the others, did not dodge fast enough and was hit full-on across his chest by the spider's large, hairy leg.

His armor shattered; the blow was that heavy. The man was thrown thirty feet away from the battle and into the thick trunk of a tree. Tar and Samson, fearing the worst for him, kept fighting on regardless.

The spider, having had some success on its left side against its many foes, decided to try its right. It brought its front right leg around and tried the same trick with Red, Gus, and Seppa. Whether it was by skill or luck, each man managed to dodge the furious blow.

"Finish him Quinn!" Tar ordered as he unsuccessfully tried to cut into the Spider's leg. Like the other Serpents on woodcutting duty, he found the Spider's exoskeleton was too thick to pierce with his blade.

Quinn realized in that moment that it was all on him and Tryan. His brothers on the ground could only distract the Voidling while they tried to slay it.

"By the Saints! Fakk!" yelled Gus above the violence as he noted a large volume of blood dripping down the human teeth of the monster. It was now or never. Quinn ripped out his short sword from the hole in the creature's exoskeleton. He brought his blade up as he was finally able to steady himself upon the fiend's head.

"Such pain . . . I feel pain . . ." said the creature with bloody teeth and gums.

"Life is pain, take this medicine," Quinn said before driving down his blade into the monster's head with all the Gift strength in him he could muster. The steel tip of his sword pierced down into the soft bug-like flesh beneath the exoskeleton and finally hit the creature's brain. As soon as that happened, the creature's legs collapsed in on themselves, unresponsive to their owner. The Serpents surrounding the Voidling leapt back as Quinn rode the toothy fiend to the ground with a heavy thud.

Quinn, sensing the Voidling was still alive although lobotomized, brought back out his blade from the wound he had made and then pierced it through again. And again as he screamed with rage! With an anger like the sun, he burned red hot! Losing himself in the violent moment, his sword broke under the continued stress of smashing at the creature underfoot.

His rage still not satisfied, he started to hammer away at its bug-like guts with his two fists, making them bloody to the bone. Not that he cared in his blind fury.

"Enough Quinn!" Tar ordered, seeing the battle frenzy that Quinn had worked himself into. "It's over, lad. It's dead."

Quinn, coming down from his battle high, breathing quick breaths, looked around at the situation in front of him. He saw Samson running toward where Bryon had landed against the tree. He wasn't moving. He then looked down at the Spider's large mouth, which Seppa, Gus, Lichale and Red now labored to get open. They feared the worst since nobody had heard a peep from Tryan since the midway point of the battle. Quinn jumped down to them as they were cutting desperately into the creature's shut mouth.

NO! It's happening again! Quinn thought in anguish as his scrapes and bruises from the fight healed themselves subtly. *Another dead body, another dead friend, another man whose death I fear witnessing above all else. Surely not him too, surely not my best friend.*

"Tryan! Tryan!" The Serpents yelled but heard no response. After a short while, they were finally able to dislodge a tooth. Utilizing the strength of them all and a claymore sword as leverage, they managed to get access to the creature's mouth, which was almost as large as a small room.

Inside they saw two things. At least a hundred cuts from Tryan's blade, causing a patter of raining blood to come down from the roof of the mouth. Then at the very back of the mouth, at the throat, they saw their brother Tryan. Ripped to pieces, almost unrecognizable. Caught on the many razor-sharp teeth that the monster had at the top of its throat cavity.

The Serpents looked at each other in despair as Samson walked back to the monster to join them, wearing the look of a man who had something he didn't want to say yet had to. The rest of the Serpents came out of the creature's mouth to meet him with an equal sadness. It started to rain.

"Bryon is gone . . ." Samson said as the heavens opened. The rain started to wash away the blood, dirt, and sweat from their stained clothes.

"So is his twin brother. Tryan is dead," Red said, starting to cry.

Quinn would have done the same but didn't. Instead, the great trauma of the moment rendered him completely dead inside. A condition, a traumatized state of mind his personal healing Gift was unable to fix. The immortal man Quinn, even though he could never die, still feared death. Why? Because it pursued his friends every day of their lives until one day, like with Bryon, Tryan, and Michael, death would finally catch them, and there was nothing he could do to stop it.

"What use is a man who can only save himself?" Quinn said so softly that none of the others likely heard him while his downcast eyes stared at his muddy boots.

"They entered this world moments apart at birth. They exit this world moments apart with their deaths," Tar said as he stepped into the conversation. "I am gladdened to know, even amid so much sadness, that whatever is beyond this life, those two will enter into it together."

Lichale, one of the few in the Akuan who still had faith in a God, said as the rain ran down his face, concealing his many tears, "They always had each other's backs in life. I'm sure it'll be the same in the afterlife. Bells, perhaps they'll even see Michael there."

"He always needed looking after too," said Red, his tears not stopping.

The Serpents looked around at each other: Tar, Samson, Red, Quinn, Lichale, Gus, and Seppa. They had started this campaign with eleven, but now they were only seven.

"What do we do now?" Quinn asked with a quiet voice as the rain poured loudly.

All the Serpents looked at each other, then at Tar. Tar said simply as he put his weatherproof hood over his head, "It's as I said before, lads. We must hope."

Chapter 7 – A Debate with Fists

Your Akuan family first, you second.
—Second Oath of the Silver Serpents

Twelve. What a perfect number that is. A perfect number of eggs, a perfect number of months, a perfect number of Akuansmen. Not too many that anyone's identity gets lost in the crowd, not too few that a foe will be able to divide and conquer you easily.

Yes, the number twelve is beloved the world over as the perfect number for an Akuan to the extent that the law even enforces it. With few exceptions given. When you see an Akuan with less than twelve members, you immediately know that something has gone awry for them.

Eleven members usually means someone was not quick enough in their last job or perhaps just got unlucky. Ten members means an unexpected event had blindsided the Akuan in a way where casualties could not be negated. Nine means that a major battle had recently transpired for the Akuan, resulting in a great tragedy.

Eight members? I've known some Akuans that wintered for an entire year in the city of Bastone just to get over the emotional cost of their losses at that number. For losing a member of one's near and dear family is traumatic and hard to get over, to say the very least.

What these men felt at only numbering seven moved them with a tragic feeling that went beyond words. For some, the tragedy brought them closer to their battle brothers, yet for others, it broke them apart.

***

The Serpents lacked options. As the Void taint spread by the Forbidden One's otherworldly dealings crept out from the epicenter of evil in the Deep Woods with each passing day, their time to stop it dwindled.

They were sure at this point that they still had not met the mastermind—their true enemy. They started calling the child and the toothy spider Heralds of the Forbidden One, as they both came prophesying the Silver Serpent's doom. But Tar did a little prophesying of his own when he ordered his Serpents with absolute resolve.

"Not one step back until we defeat the fiend. Until we arrive at the very center of all this pain. This started in the Deep Woods, and we'll end it there. Even if it costs us everything, we shall end this for us and for all."

So, going where no sane man or woman has ever tried to venture before, a place at the very center of the Deep Woods where an alien dimension is said to brush up against our own, the Serpents picked themselves up by their muddy bootstraps and went onward. Thinking that whatever horrific monster lay at the top of the hierarchy of otherworldly horrors in the Deep Woods must be their unknown nemesis, it was one last time that they had to venture into the breach of hell. With the deaths of Michael and the twins Bryon and Tryan, the final part of their campaign against the Forbidden One had just commenced.

They trekked on through the swamp for two days as the rain poured down their wet faces, as their boots filled with swamp water and muck, becoming heavier by the moment. In all that time, they were unable to properly make a camp to rest, so every night was spent with the feeling of cold rain upon them. Eventually, they reached the Swamp of Woman Who Unceremoniously Went Away. A week ago, they were joking merrily about its name, but now they weren't. The rainstorms had transformed it into a quagmire of watery death; they weren't wading through it anymore, they had to swim instead.

Their gear was worn and waterlogged. Their arrows were all spent on the increasing number of Voidlings they found along their path to doom incarnate. Their blades were in dire need of a blacksmith's grinding stone from so much continual use.

The mood was almost mutinous when they came to an island of mud in the sea of swamps. Without a word needed between them, they chose to take residence there in hope of resting from their exhaustion, if only for a few precious hours or so.

Quinn, still the point man, swam ashore, but when he tried to stand up on the mud, he slipped. Gravity and tiredness helped the mud force him back onto his knees, as if nature itself was making him kneel before its grandeur.

Quinn took off his waterlogged boots and found himself better able to stand on his bare feet on this almost holy ground, anointed by nature to be the only thing within sight above the flooded water level of the swamp.

Quinn helped his brothers up and out of the swamp water after him. Many fell as he did when they tried to stand on the slippery mud. Rainwater trickled down on them via a thousand leaves overhead. Even with the dense mangrove canopy above, there was no dry place to be found, and so they had to live like aquatic beings. Always cold, always wet.

"I swear this swamp is trying to drown us," said Seppa as he and his brothers finally all got ashore. Exhaustion from the hours of swimming and wading now getting to them all, they collapsed upon the mud of the "island."

Quinn noted belly-slide imprints of alligators that were likely using this small ten-by-ten-yard island as a respite. He didn't say anything about it though, because if anything did try to reclaim this "holy" ground, then it would soon be turned into lunch for seven very hungry men.

"I guess there isn't much point in trying to start a fire," said Gus as he sat in the mud across from the rest of the men now forming an exhausted circle.

"We don't have anything left to cook. The flour has gone all moldy and wet. I've completely lost all my cooking utensils," said Lichale in a monotone.

"I lost the fishing bait a day ago, I reckon," said Red, as down as they all were. Even old man Tar was showing some signs of emotional exhaustion, let alone his physical pain, which he hid with great effort so as not to worry his younger, stronger Akuan brothers.

"We have little hope of catching anything anyway. Swamp fish don't come to the surface during a storm this heavy," said Seppa, the expert on local game. He had trained as a Danneishie Ranger in his youth in an attempt to follow in the footsteps of his late father.

"They'd probably just be filled with Void parasites like all the other animals we've tried to eat since the village," said Quinn, stating what was now obvious to them all.

"Look at you all, so inherently depressed that a little bout of bad weather is getting you down. I thought you men called yourselves tough," said Samson as he grinned half-heartedly, trying to stir some emotion other than despair from his men, who responded like walking corpses. They wallowed in depression, hunger, and exhaustion—transfixed by the sight of their wet, muddy boots.

"Where is your bravado, men? You lot have all the enthusiasm for life as a rock," said Tar, trying to draw the complaints of his men out of them so those thoughts would not devour them from the inside.

"Our bravado, sir?" Gus shook his head dismissively as rainwater poured down his messy, balding hairline. "Ha . . . ha . . . ha. What a joke . . . You ordered us to cease our bravado when we found that dead Ranger who was dropped from the sky upon the Sea of Reeds, remember, sir?"

All the men looked at Tar, who had obviously forgotten that fact, most likely due to his age, which lent itself to forgetfulness in even good circumstances, let alone a bad one like this.

"If you've got something to say, Akuansmen, say it," said Samson with seriousness as he didn't like Gus's disrespectful tone.

"Not another fight. We don't need this," Quinn said as he lay back onto the mud, not caring at this point in the slightest how dirty it made him.

"Shut the fakk up Quinn. Let the full Serpents speak their peace," Red said to Quinn as it became apparent that Red was as mad as Gus.

The Serpents went quiet as they realized the atmosphere of the moment had changed. Calling out a brother, even a probationary one, with swear words was directly against the spirit of Oaths Four and Two, meaning that among the Silver Serpents, Red's offhand comments were fighting words.

Quinn sat up quickly and saw Tar and Samson staring down Red and Gus with intimidation in their tired expressions. Seppa, seeing this too, tried to de-escalate the situation by saying, "Quinn may be impervious to common sense and good manners a lot of the time, but brother, he doesn't deserve any disrespect. You hear?"

"Aye, take back the comment," Lichale added.

"Sorry, Quinn," Red said while looking Tar directly in the eye. "I didn't mean to take out my rage on you. It's meant for somebody else . . ."

"Hear, fakkin' hear, mate," said Gus as he too stared down Tar, who didn't flinch.

He just smiled back at them both, saying, "It seems that even in the depths of watery hell, idiots like you two will still try to fight with your battle brothers. If I was but ten years younger, I would throw you both to the alligators and fish."

"But you aren't ten years younger, right? You are just an old man with only a few more years left in 'im. Hell bent on a last hurrah into glory at the price of your men's lives," said Red with a deep-seated anger that had grown within the recent days of turmoil from the seed that was his natural distrust of authority.

"Careful, Serpent. Using bad logic makes you actively dumber," said Tar, his death stare now intensifying to something like what a villain would wear.

"The smarter I get, the unhappier I become," said Gus in retort, obviously siding with Red in what was now a battle of egos more than anything.

"You've both just insulted our commander to his face, lads. Despite these extenuating circumstances, that is not something that can be overlooked," said Samson in an uncharacteristic low, growling voice he would only use when diplomacy looked like a failing option.

"Our discipline is the only thing keeping us alive, you idiots. De'far!" Swore Seppa, his rage directed at Gus and Red. Like Tar and Samson, he was pissed off by them as well. Lichale, like Quinn, just sat on the sidelines. Watching.

"How are you going to pay for these transgressions, lads?" said Samson, wearing the mantle of Fredstar the Sergeant in this situation.

"I'm going to mitosis myself into two, then blame the other guy," Red said with a cheeky grin as Gus laughed at Red's bad joke, even though he didn't know what the word mitosis meant.

Not taking the joke kindly, Tar said, "Come on then, out with it! Say the words that you've been trying to find the courage to say for these last two days." Tar looked into the eyes of Red and Gus like he already knew their business without having to be told. Understanding in the moment what Tar was speaking about, Red was about to speak his peace when Gus interrupted him.

"How can you still hope for our victory?! How can you believe that we will overcome this?! Can you not bloody see what we have already lost?! Can you not see who is missing by our sides? You too Quinn, you're as bad as Tar in your delusions. Honestly, how can you both sit there and tell me there is a way forward when everyone can clearly see there is not?"

"Cynicism and nihilism are the mental language of idiots who think they know everything, my world-weary friends. Don't count yourself one of their perpetually unhappy number. Hope for the best, prepare for the worst, but be joyful regardless, I say," said Lichale in defense of his commander, having now picked a side. As the rain poured and their stomachs ached with hunger, the men all went silent.

Red finally grunted out a laugh at Lichale's words. To the well fed, warm, and safe, those words would have seemed like wisdom, but to the starving, cold, and afraid, they were an unfunny fairy tale. A joke masquerading as wisdom.

"Actually, you're right Gus. There is nothing to have hope in, yet I still have faith we will win. You want to know my secret?" Tar said before leaving a pause, which nobody filled. "You want to know why Quinn and I, and even Samson and Lichale now as well, still believe, despite all the evidence to the contrary, that we shall win? It's because we've decided it so. When there is no hope to be seen or heard, it can only be imagined."

"So, you admit it then? You are delusional," Gus said as if Tar's words were the final straw to break within him.

"He's not delusional. He's just choosing to be brave, you idiot," said Seppa, acting like he was too good for all this arguing.

As Red flicked a mosquito from his face and then ran his hand through his hair, his green-eyed stare to Tar said one thing: this is over. He then looked to Gus, who nodded back, prompting him to say determinedly, "We are leaving, sir. Give us an honorable discharge from the Akuan. We'll find our own way out of this mess. Anyone who wants to come with us is welcome to."

"How about no," Tar said softly. Samson stood in anger, fists clenched at his side as Red and Gus, the two brawlers, did the same.

"Think carefully now lads. We ain't giving anyone an easy way out," Samson said as he cracked his knuckles.

"You won't dishonorably discharge us. You aren't that cold-blooded," Gus said, calling Samson's bluff.

"No, we won't. But we'll give you two milk-drinking, turncoat bastards what you deserve," said Tar, looking up from his relaxed position on the ground.

"Seppa. Won't you help me teach these men a lesson in their own stupidity?" said Samson as he eyed a slightly taken aback Red and Gus, who hadn't expected a physical altercation over this.

"Sir, I can't hurt my brothers, whatever the case. Not again," said Seppa as he remained seated, his mind going back to the event that saw Fredstar's death.

"Same with me sir," said Lichale, taking the easy way out.

"What about you Quinn? I see you still sit there. Whose side are you taking?" asked Samson.

"My own. I'm still an outsider here, remember?" Samson shook his head with a smile at Quinn's words.

"Technically, you're right, but at the same time . . . you're wrong. Help me," Samson asked.

"No, you don't need it," said Quinn, to which Samson breathed out a sigh.

"You're not a very empathetic person, are you?" Samson said as he alone stared down the two younger and physically stronger Red and Gus, as Tar would be useless in a physical altercation.

"I'm empathetic enough. I can understand and feel emotions like anyone else. My problem is I don't care whether Gus or Red leave now. I think we'll be able to best the Forbidden One with or without these cowards."

"Shut your fakkin' mouth, you don't know nothing Quinn," said Gus.

"Well then, it seems I won't be able to share the fun with anyone," Samson said before quickly moving in on the two younger men so fast that it took them both by surprise.

Gus, the closer of the two rebels, swung in with his fist, but Samson, knowing his moves better than even he did, easily dodged the blow and came in close with his own. Using a technique of bare-knuckle boxing known only to him and his brother, who died long ago, he came in faster than a man over fifty should be able to.

What confused Gus and made him unable to block was Samson's choice of target. Gus was expecting that once Samson got past his brawler's guard, he'd go for his head. So he ducked to miss an incoming blow there. But Samson wasn't aiming for that. He was going for the real, lesser-known weak point of the human body. The best place to punch someone is the liver, not the head, as your body can't handle it nearly as well.

A single moment was all it took before Gus, after receiving a heavy blow there, was on the muddy ground in great pain. Red took no time to further argue his point. He just roared, then charged with abandon at Samson, who had put down his accomplice way easier than he expected.

Thinking his best chance was to use his body weight against the weaker, less agile man, Red threw himself onto Samson. But Samson had something Red didn't—a wealth of fighting experience that went back decades. He was a master; Red was a student.

Samson twisted in the mud as he slid aside of Red's charge. The mud caked onto Samson's clothes was so slippery that Red wasn't able to grab onto him. Samson used Red's momentum to fling him into a somersault and then onto the ground with a wet, muddy splash, all in one graceful, fluid movement. Samson pulled out a finishing blade from his boot, then put it to Red's throat as he knelt over him.

"You want to continue, lad? You think I won't kill you for being a coward?! The way I see it, you two running away when we need you both is as good as being an accessory to our deaths. You are either working for us or the Forbidden One. Make your choice!" Samson yelled, reminding Red, who was at his whim, that there were other forces in this swamp that he needed to fear. In particular, him.

Red turned his head and saw a now unconscious Gus. The punch to his liver had lowered both his heart rate and blood pressure to the degree that his body went into survival mode, rendering him momentarily unconscious. His fellow rebel was down for the count. His plan to leave had failed before it even really started.

"Bells! You see that?" Lichale said, standing up while gazing into the distance. All eyes except Red's, who was not able to look where Lichale was pointing because he was pinned to the ground, followed Lichale's finger. They all saw in the distance as the rain continued to pour down without relenting, a purple fog drifting their way.

"UVE incoming!" Quinn yelled, causing Samson to jump off Red and both men to stand at the ready against this new, mutual threat.

In the commotion of violence and argument, none had seen the UVE creeping toward them. It was only a hundred yards away from them. It made no sound that could be heard over the constant pouring rain. Stretching east and west as far as the eye could see, this UVE did not seem escapable. At all.

"This UVE . . . I've survived one of these before. There are Voidlings inside that artificial fog. This is their hunting technique, you see. Do what I say exactly, and you'll all live," said Tar with authority.

All the men in the Akuan looked to Tar, who now simply sat on the ground instead of getting ready for battle. Legs crossed in the mud, he looked as if he was about to meditate rather than prepare for a fight with whatever Voidlings were concealing themselves in this unnatural weather formation.

"Do what I'm doing. Sit in this pose. Form a circle, all of you, quick! We can't hope to face what's inside that; we'll need to sneak through," Tar said as his men did what they were told without questioning as there was no time. All except Gus, who was still unconscious, and Red, who still had his doubts about Tar. And so he stood alone with his sword out.

"What about Gus?" Samson said as he took up his position next to his commander.

"He'll be fine. He has the best chance of making it through out of all of us. That is, so long as he doesn't wake up midway through."

Red, upon seeing that all his brothers were taking Tar's words as fact and because he could not think of any better way of tackling the situation, finally sat down like the rest of them in a circle. The purple fog was now fifty yards away and closing.

"Listen carefully, lads. Do everything I tell you to the letter, and you'll live. Anything less, and you'll die. The beings in this cloud cannot see, so they hunt based on movement. Do not move other than to breathe lightly. If they touch you, and it is likely that they will as we smell like prey, absolutely do not respond. No matter how much your survival instinct may say otherwise," Tar said adamantly.

"Act like a tree or a rock. Got it," Samson said, summarizing for his men. Lichale gulped as he looked at the dense purple fog that was now only twenty yards away and closing.

"Shut your eyes lads, and keep them closed. It'll be easier to not react if you can't see them. If you see them for but a moment, you'll want to flinch. You flinch but a little bit, and they'll figure you out as their prey and take you with them."

"Sir, how will we know when it's over?" asked Quinn with his eyes shut.

"Unlike you all, I'll keep my eyes open. I'll let you know. At best this will only take a few minutes, at worst a few hours. So don't move, eyes closed, breathe lightly and steadily. You hear me Serpents?!" Tar exclaimed.

"Yes, sir!' said his men. Even Red, although his came a little later. The men waited patiently for the fog to hit them. Their nerves were high and their hearts pounding hard. After five minutes of nervously waiting for something to happen, the men realized that the front of the purple fog must already be upon them. Yet they felt nothing, only the rain.

For Quinn, the worst part was the not knowing, the waiting for something to touch him at any moment but not knowing where and when. Would it feel rough? Wet? Slimy? What does the grasp of this alien feel like? He feared that when it touched him, his natural fight-or-flight survival instincts would kick in, resulting in an unwanted body movement that would get him killed or worse, taken. Whatever that entailed.

This encounter made him realize that the worst kind of threat you can face is that of the unknown. Despite these fears, which made him deeply uncomfortable, he sat perfectly still as he and the rest of the Serpents trusted Tar that they would survive if they did what they were told. That is, except one.

Out of seemingly nowhere, Quinn felt clawed hands move over his body. Something began touching him, poking him, testing him with purposeful force. He gritted his teeth as he realized that the alien was acting not like an animal but like a sentient being, which made it all the more dangerous.

With three fingers on each of its four hands, the Voidling tried to understand the shape of the man in front of it by feeling around with its itch-inducing palms. Across his arms, across his legs, then even his face. It groped its surroundings like a blind man making his way through a house he had never been in before.

But Quinn was calm and endured this with trained discipline and resolve for forty-five long seconds before one of his brothers broke the otherworldly silence of the terrible moment.

"Arrgh! Get off me! Get off me—"

His brother's loud voice suddenly was cut off. As soon as Quinn had heard those words, the alien departed from him. He sensed it rushing toward the brother who had revealed himself as their prey. There was more than one of these beings in the fog, it seemed. Bells, there could have been hundreds for all the Serpents knew.

Quinn waited for a while but heard nothing more than rain. It was as if whoever made the mistake of struggling against the being of the Void was no longer there and thus could not be heard. As he sat in perfect silence for fifteen more heart-rending minutes, he was glad that the alien did not seem to want to return to him.

"Serpents, it's clear," said Tar with a heavy sense of regret. Quinn opened his eyes, as did they all, to see what happened to the man who cried out in fear amid the now passed danger. To the man who broke perfect discipline when it was the only thing between him and his untimely death.

It was their brother Red, as Quinn had suspected from the sound of his voice. The red-haired, green-eyed former thief who always had a complaint ready had complained his last. Red's body and gear were gone, like he was abducted to another world. And perhaps he was. The only thing left was the soft imprint in the mud his butt had made, which was now pooling with rainwater.

The Serpents looked at each other, heartbroken, without any more words needed between them. They were now down to only six, the lowest number the Akuan had ever known in its one-hundred-plus-year history.

This tragedy, this breakdown of the Akuan family measured in dead bodies would change them forever, they realized in that speechless moment. Gus suddenly woke up from unconsciousness and sat up, showing soreness in his side.

"Argh fakk me . . . Of course, ya bloody do me a dirty," Gus said as he shook himself awake then looked around at all the serious, despondent faces. Understanding that something bad had just happened, he asked a question nobody wanted to answer.

"Brothers, where's Red?"

Chapter 8 – This Time with More Feeling

The next day.

As the sun boiled down unseasonably, the Silver Serpents, now numbering only six vipers, finally shed their skin of cowardice once and for all. When they entered the Sea of Reeds on that ninth day of the campaign they were waging against the Forbidden One, the point of no return was long gone. For the Void had corrupted the swampland and bogs with its alien presence, from the outskirts of the Deep Woods all the way to Parika' Te Mo.

To go back now was as dangerous as venturing forward. Venturing forward was now as dangerous as staying put, as evidenced by what happened to Red. Yes, now that their back was clearly against the wall, conventional logic caught up to the conclusion that Tar's blind hope had found days ago. Their only hope was to go forth and slay whatever being was at the center of all this tragic mess.

The Serpents trekked through the Sea of Reeds in water up to their ankles, having accepted but not made peace with the shadow of death that loomed heavily over them. Luckily, the rainstorms had halted and been replaced supernaturally by waves of heat, which evaporated the water buildup from days before.

What was cold and wet yesterday was now humid and dry. It was clear that the Void was adversely affecting the local weather. As if a new resident was changing the habitat to match its own tastes, the swamplands were disappearing before their eyes. What was it going to be replaced with? That terrible question was what no Serpent had a mind to ask.

While the point man, Quinn, cut through the Sea of Reeds with a blunt hatchet, the reeds in their millions swayed in the wind that had been created by a southernly sea breeze, a breeze that cooled off the profusely sweating Serpents. It was now the only thing still normal about the weather.

Known in the area as the blue man's bellow (as it originates from the grumpy old man known as the Sea of Blues), it helped to guide the Serpents north. In the direction of what, in the distance, now looked like an alien landscape. The Deep Woods had been thus so corrupted in mere days.

Like the ships that sail on the Sea of Blues yet arrive at disaster on jagged rocks or dangerous waves, never to be seen or heard from again, the Serpents ventured on a collision course with death that would have them find the final Herald foretold in Pell's tall tale. On that ninth day of the campaign against the Forbidden One, it finally became apparent how many Akuansmen's lives this single Voidling was worth.

***

"If Tar says it can be done, it can. That's what I believe," said Lichale to his brothers as they trekked in single file among the nine-foot-high reeds. Gus, the man this statement was squarely directed at, just bit his lip, not bothering to utter a word as he knew he was condemned to whatever fate had in store for them. So why argue against it then? he probably thought.

"He's right, you know Gus. Now that I think about it, Tar has never led us on a campaign that didn't see its ultimate goal fulfilled," said Seppa, wiping the sweat off his brow as he watched the blue sky above for any threats. Glancing down occasionally as he followed the point man Quinn at the head of the Serpent procession, he was cautious like they all were, but at least he felt himself again.

"We'll see the other side of this, lads. I swear it," Samson said as he helped an ailing Tar along, who had twisted his ankle just a

101

few hours before to the point he could no longer walk by himself.

"The way I see it, while the Forbidden One has trapped us in its growing domain by forces unknown, it has also unified us against it like never before. Something I know for sure our foe does not want," said Quinn as he slashed a path through the reeds where previously there was none.

"Hear, hear," said Tar, Samson, Lichale, and Seppa, all agreeing with Quinn's notion.

"Look at all you bloody idiots. We got nothing but blunt blades and good vibes, and you are still acting like you own the show 'round here," said Gus, not as merry minded as the others, who had all decided to believe in the impossible and were all the better for it.

"My blade may be blunt, but my dagger is still sharp!" roared Lichale.

"Hear, hear!" said the Serpents, excluding Gus, as their spirits lifted. Gus shook his head with a smile as he fell victim to his brothers' enthusiasm, which had been absent for days until now.

"We are going to do this for Fredstar. For Tryan and Bryon. Mikey and Red. For those thirty families lost in Parika' Te Mo. And if we can't avenge them. If the worst happens and we fail, we'll join them in the afterlife, where we'll meet not only them but all the Silver Serpents who have ever perished. There we shall rejoice with them eternally. The way I see it, to live is gain, but to die is gain also," Tar said with a confident smile.

"Hear, hear," said Lichale, the only other nonagnostic among them.

"Hope there's more than a few beers in the afterlife. If I die horribly, Imma wanna forget it," Gus said, to which his brothers grinned.

"If I die horribly, I think I'll—"

"BLLLLLLLLAHHHHHHHHKKKKKKKKKK!"

A loud cry that screamed in their heads from seemingly all directions at the same time cut Samson's sentence. The Serpents knew what it was. They had heard it seven days ago. The group crouched and tried to hide among the reeds. They were taking no chances this time.

"That Voidling is back at it. Still sounds like nothing I've heard before," said Seppa.

"Anyone got eyes on it?" asked Gus.

"No. But whatever it is, it sounds big," answered Quinn, not sure whether he should be scanning the blue, cloudless sky or the sea of reeds all around them for an incoming threat.

"What should we expect? It's about time for the third Herald in Pell's story. What did he describe it as? A big rainbow bird with no head but eyes all over its underside?" Lichale said.

"Yes, but he didn't describe it having a mouth. This thing obviously does if it can produce a warning cry that loud," Samson said.

"Lads," Tar said, collapsed in Samson's arms, ready to be lifted out of harm's way if necessary. "This creature isn't using sound for its warning cry. It's using telepathy. It wouldn't need a mouth for that."

"Wait, so I'm not actually hearing anything? It's all in my head?" asked Seppa, to which Tar nodded.

"Well that explains why it sounds so bloody close," said Gus.

"A Voidling using telepathy to warn away prey from its territory? What does this strange behavior suggest?" asked Lichale.

"It means that the third Herald is sentient like the other two and that it is simply trying to intimidate us away. Think about it. Each Herald up until now has tried to push us further away from the Deep Woods, not closer," said Quinn, turning back to his brothers behind him to explain his deduction.

"Quinn is correct. The Forbidden One is not only aware of the threat we pose but is fearfully trying to keep us away. We are going the right way," Tar said, then gestured for the Akuan to resume its pace forward.

"I guess if the Forbidden One thinks there is still a chance we could kill it, and so it's hunting us down, it must mean there really is a chance for us to slay it. Otherwise, it would simply not bother," said Samson, connecting the dots.

"Hear, hear," said his brothers in good cheer, finding this news very pleasing indeed.

"See, Gus. Even the Forbidden One agrees that there is a chance we can kill it. You must be the only one in these lands to think otherwise," said Lichale as his brothers grinned.

"Ha fakkin' ha, boys. If our brother Red had not just died, maybe I'd be laughing with ya," Gus said, bringing everyone's mood down.

After a while of quiet striding through the ankle-deep water in the considerable heat as the sun above boiled away, the Serpents exhausted the remainder of their fresh water supply, something that was unthinkable a few days ago.

"Quinn, are we almost out of the Reed Sea by your reckoning? We need to boil some more drinking water soon; otherwise, we'll all collapse from thirst," said Lichale.

"Don't forget food. We need more to fill our bellies than a few frogs and wild berries if we are to battle the Forbidden One," said Seppa, still watching the skies as he followed in Quinn's footsteps.

"We are almost out. It's not much longer till . . ." Sensing the rushing of air along the tops of the reeds, Quinn realized something was moving toward them. He stopped and looked back just in time to see Seppa uprooted from the ground and swiftly taken by two massive bird claws. Each was the size of a six-foot man.

It happened so quickly, so silently. If you did not see the sight of the rainbow-feathered hawk-like bird without a beak or head come by and take him, you would have thought Seppa was simply spirited away from this world without a trace. But it was not so. Effortlessly parting reeds as it strafed along the ground, the third and final Herald made its presence known as a snatcher of men.

Seppa screamed for help as the rainbow bird, covered in a hundred horrific-looking red, green, and purple eyes on its underside, lifted him higher into the air with every flap of its long, seventy-yard wingspan. His brothers soon realized they could do nothing to aid him. For, just as yesterday, they had no arrows to fell a flighted foe.

They were silent, all watching the third Herald fly out of earshot with their brother in its grasp, high above the Sea of Reeds. Their hearts jumped out of their mouths when they saw the sentient Voidling unceremoniously drop Seppa at the apex of its climb, from a height most mountains don't reach.

"Quinn, put me on your back and carry me out of here. Rest of you, split up and make it to the thick overhead cover in the Deep Woods. We can only hope it'll take more time to acquire its next target if we separate," Tar ordered as all the men watched the Herald, having dropped Seppa to his death, turn around in the air, then tuck its wings close to its body to begin yet another quick dive. A dive in their direction.

"Quick lads! There is no way we can fight it! We must head for the tall trees! It's our only defense!" yelled Tar, rousting his men into action. They were almost stupefied by what they saw happen just a few terrifying moments before. Something they all saw clearly yet could do nothing about. The Herald had not only taken their brother in a single moment but also their bravado. They stood there feeling completely helpless.

"We're gonna make it, lads. Get with it!" Tar yelled as he tried to hobble over to Quinn but soon fell. Quinn, waking up from his shock, caught the old man in his arms, then swung him around onto his back, realizing they had no time to think on what had just happened.

"You heard him Serpents! Split up! Head north till you hit the outskirts of the Deep Woods," ordered Samson as the rest of the men came back to their senses, their shock removed by a combination of life-threatening urgency and well-drilled discipline.

"Quinn and I will make a campfire. Look for our smoke. Form up on us by nightfall," Tar ordered as he and his Serpents all looked at each other with immense worry. Gus, Samson, Lichale, Tar, and Quinn—each man somehow sensed that this would be the last time they would all be together, and they halted as one as if trying to memorize the details of each other's faces. To etch into stone what could be the last time they saw their brothers alive.

The moment soon over, the Serpents split up without any further words. Each man chose a way through the reeds that looked promising. Quinn departed with Tar firmly on his back, as both men knew that, out of all of them, despite one being unable to walk, they had the best chance of surviving this aerial onslaught from a foe they could not best.

Tar and Quinn, knowing each other's dangerous secret, were finally out of view of their brothers and could use their supernatural Gifts freely. The very Gifts that made them so hated were now the only hope to save their lives. Yes, Tar was like Quinn—a Rogue Caster hiding within a Rogue-Caster-hunting Akuan. Yes, you heard me. The most prestigious group of Rogue Caster hunters on the whole continent was led by a man who was their natural enemy. A man whose personal history demanded his lawful death.

Had Tar's brothers, excluding Quinn, known this truth then, not one of them would have followed him anywhere, let alone let him continue to live. Yet they did not know and so, in their ignorance, followed what they hated. Just like with Quinn, they loved the man only because they didn't know what he really was. That was the basis of Quinn and Tar's special bond. That was how they could so easily trust each other with their lives; they practiced that trust daily.

"Sir, can you read its mind this time?" Quinn asked as he pushed his Caster energy, often described as inner warmth, to his legs, which were then supernaturally strengthened, enabling him to run through the reeds faster than a regular man, despite the extra load on his back.

"No. Its thoughts are not in a language I know, just like the others. Nor in a paradigm I think my human mind can even comprehend. It is indeed alien, yet I sense something more, something strangely nonvoidling within it. Almost as if it's real but not real at the same time. Like the other two Heralds' existences, it makes no sense to me," Tar said questioningly as he used his Caster power to try and read the mind of the aerial fiend.

Quinn ran through the ankle-deep water with abandon. He made his way through walls of reeds with no hatchet, only supernatural brute strength alone. Old man Tar, feeling his age, held dearly onto Quinn. Not having a Cast other than mind reading, he could do little to aid his only chance of escape.

"Duck!" Tar yelled. And Quinn immediately dove onto the watery ground. Quinn turned his head to the side a moment later, the full weight of Tar still on his back. He saw the feathered tail of the rainbow bird disappear behind the trail of disturbed reeds it left in its wake. There was no telling how close the two had just come to being snatched away.

In a quick moment, they were back up and running. Running for their lives. One keeping watch through psychic means, the other like a beast of burden galloping them both to safety.

"How are the others?" Quinn asked through heavy breaths as he ran northward as best he could.

"Samson's dead. Not sure about the other two. They are out of my Gift's range," Tar said calmly as Quinn gritted his teeth in anger.

"Can we not do something for them?!" Quinn asked in his mind, knowing that Tar could read his thoughts as easily as any other's.

"No, we cannot save them. They can only save themselves," Tar said softly.

Quinn used his inner voice to talk back to him, saying, "Had we fought together, could we not have prevailed? I could have used my Gifts and—"

"What? Saved them? If you did, I would have had to order you killed on the spot, you do realize? Regardless of if we won or not. Besides, in our current condition, even with your Gift's utilized, we would have failed. This Herald is just too large and fast. We'd need at least eleven Akuansmen to fell it, and even then, that strength would be better utilized killing the Forbidden One. We should avoid this one for now."

It was at this moment that Quinn, while carrying Tar on his back, finally broke through the Sea of Reeds and into the waist-high waters of a blackened marsh that was not there before.

The two men stopped in their tracks as they gazed in horror at the otherworldly landscape that had appeared before them. It was as if Mother Nature had become diseased and cancerous, with hairy boils and puss-filled wounds hanging off now purple-leaved, blackened trees.

The forest, once rich in dark green undergrowth, was now rich in a skin-like substance, which replaced the green terrain with a dark, hairy moss. The new alien environment was more horrific up close than it appeared from afar. The very Deep Woods itself had become a single alien organism.

"Forward! It's closing!" yelled Tar. Quinn didn't need to be told twice. He waded as quickly as he could through the blackened marsh, which seemed to ooze oil and . . . blood?

"How close is it? I'm not going to make it through this bog in—"

"Too late!" exclaimed Tar as Quinn felt something hit him like a hammer.

He was flung into the marsh to his left side; his head went underneath the waist-high mix of oil, mud, and alien blood. Quickly pulling his head up from the foul, murky liquid, he saw the rainbow bird, adorned with a hundred creepy eyes, drop a mere thirty yards away the man it had stolen from his back. The aerial fiend then continued its climb, up and away.

Quinn rushed over to his commander and pulled him out of the strange, otherworldly liquid. Covered in its foul muck as badly as Quinn was, Tar got situated once more onto Quinn's back.

"Quickly! To shore. I blasted it with my mind, a burst of all-encompassing emotion so dark and fearful that a normal man would have committed suicide on the spot to escape from it. But it's in no way a normal anything; it'll soon come back."

Quinn and Tar rushed ashore through the black marsh and into the living forest now covered in horrific, alien flesh. After a few moments of running, they could no longer see the sky, only the purple leaves above. Only then did they feel safe from the third Herald.

Yet at the same time, they knew they had simply traded one enemy for another. For the Deep Woods, as they could see all around them, had just gotten a lot more dangerous.

Chapter 9 – A Moment of Ostentation

Be kind to the stranger, the wayfarer, the unknown quantity along the journey. For good is rewarded with good, and absence of mercy is rewarded in turn.
—Fifth Oath of the Silver Serpent

With great tiredness upon them, Quinn and Tar sat beside a campfire that barely burned at the edge of the Deep Woods, at a small haven of the human world that the strange, alien skin had not grown over, yet.

There, under the cover of tall trees, the two men sat without words in almost complete darkness for hours. The screams and roars of strange, never-before-heard-of Voidlings filled their ears and souls well into the chilly night.

Quinn thought that it must have been three or four hours or so past midnight by the time either of them uttered a single word. It was well past the nightfall deadline that was given to the rest of the Serpents to regroup on them. Had anyone else survived the Sea of Reeds encounter, they were supposed to follow the scent of smoke, the light of a campfire. But now that campfire, which burned on for hours, just like their hope, was finally giving up.

"Commander . . ." Quinn said, unsure if the old man before him had finally drifted to sleep.

"Yes Quinny?" said Tar, not opening his eyes, looking older in the flickering light of the dwindling campfire than Quinn had ever seen him before.

"Can I ask you something, sir?"

"It seems that all we have left now is our questions. Ask away."

"I know it may seem stupid to ask this with all that's going on that's more important, but why? Why did you never tell me Sae was really our prey in disguise? Thinking back on it now, I don't think I ever really knew the woman I once claimed to love. But you did. You read her mind and yet . . ."

"Yet I did not tell you she was that kind of trouble? Had I told you, you still would have chosen her as your companion anyway. I can read your mind as well as hers." Tar smiled with his eyes still shut, his body hunched over toward the campfire for warmth, to keep the chill away from his old bones.

Quinn and Tar sat in silence for a while, "enjoying" more sounds of hungry unknown monsters in the near distance. Voidling's they knew they'd have to deal with come morn.

"I promised you, didn't I? That one day I'd tell you everything you want to know, laddie. About her, about you, about me. About your troubled past, which you still do not remember," Tar said, continuing his thought from before.

"Yet today is not that day?!" Quinn all but shouted. "Let me remind you, Commander, there is only one immortal man here, and it's me. If I am burnt to ash by the Forbidden One, I will rise again in fifty years without knowledge of who I was before, such is my Gift, such is my curse. You, sir . . . I fear that you are going to die here! And your secret knowledge of my past self with you. There is only one other that knew me fifty years ago. From before I awoke from a mass grave. I can't afford to lose either of you. If that happens, I fear I'll never reclaim who I was before."

Tar chuckled at Quinn's outburst.

"What are you laughing at?" an offended Quinn said, to which Tar finally opened his eyes. He smiled lightly with alien muck still on half of his wrinkled face.

"So, you've finally given up hope too. You lasted longer than the others. I'll give you that. But then again, you are just like me, aren't you? Just don't have the wisdom that comes with age yet."

"What are you talking about?"

"We are both killing machines, Quinn," Tar sighed. "Like the denizens of this otherworldly forest, we are creatures of horror, monsters in human form. We are natural apex killers. Such is the original purpose of us mutants, us Casters, whether Rogue or otherwise. It's why people hate us.

"Some say Casters were made to fight the Void. Others say we were created by it. Who is correct? Probably both. I guess it's only fitting in a quiet, sad way that we end our lives with the rest of the horrors of this world. Here in this godforsaken place. We fit in nicely, I say, even though we are not welcome guests."

Quinn was shocked by Tar's candid words. He no longer spoke to Quinn as a subordinate but as an equal. A friend. Quinn shook his head in despair, a despair that had been building long before the words *Forbidden One* were ever uttered.

"Yet I am worse still. I am a weapon that cannot be retired, unlike my now dead battle brothers. What a sad joke it is that the only immortal man in existence, one who should have no fear of death, is yet terrified of it still. For I find myself obsessed with the death of others I held dear."

"Would you give anything to see them again?" Tar asked soberly, to which Quinn nodded.

Tar then sighed heavily before he said, "The curse of immortality, my friend, may still see us to our victory. You alone are likely the real reason the Forbidden One feared our Akuan and so tried to break us. I suspect it picked off our brothers one by one in the style that it did because it wished to break your resolve to kill it, through the burden of sadness. Of which I see evidence now on your face."

Quinn looked down, ashamed of himself, realizing Tar was right. With the almost certain deaths of his unaccounted-for brothers Lichale and Gus, he had given up hope not just in victory over their foe but in the worth of that victory itself. Even if they killed the Forbidden One now, who would be left to celebrate it? The answer . . . almost no one.

"Is victory worth everything you have? Everything you hold dear? That is the question I have continually been asking myself."

"And?" Quinn asked, looking up from his boots at a serious, green-eyed stare from Tar.

"If it means defeating evil, defeating humanity's greatest foe, the Void. Then yes. For that is an Akuan's purpose in life, is it not? To beat back the Void from our world for but one more day."

"Yes, so it is."

"Then all our brothers who have seen us thus far with their lives died for something. They died getting us this far. Getting you back here. And so it will be that my death also shall get you one step further than you are."

Quinn looked at Tar with great confusion. He looked down at Tar's body in the darkness, and he saw something he had overlooked before. Tar was covered in alien blood just as he was, but Tar was covered in human blood as well—his own.

"Are you dying?"

Tar smiled back at his last remaining Akuan brother.

"Yes, my friend. It seems you are correct. I am not much longer for this bittersweet world."

Tar, finally giving into his pain, fell over onto his side. His wound, once concealed by his arm, was now obvious for Quinn to see. The third Herald, when it had plucked Tar from Quinn's back with its large claws, had left Tar with a parting gift—a wound they had no way of treating. Quinn had no words to say as he rushed over to cradle his dying mentor and counterpart. For in that moment, he realized his greatest fear was imminent. Not that of the Forbidden One, but that of being in a cruel, twisted war waged against an unknown foe, all alone.

"Akuan life never gets boring, does it?" Tar jokily said, showing little visible pain as he lay on his side. Resting his head on a now seated Quinn.

"What should I do? How will I go on?" Quinn said as his always-tough exterior finally broke.

"Let's just talk. You don't have to do anything but listen."

"Tar, if you are really dying, you must tell me all that you know. Of my past, of Sae . . . Everything."

"No Quinny, you are still not ready to hear what I have to say. The answers I have for you . . . the answers to important questions that kept you in this Akuan even though you really wished to leave with Sae the moment she confessed her love to you, those answers shall die with me. For I fear that if I reveal them to you now in your tortured state of mind, it'll destroy you in a moment when you need to be strong."

Quinn realized Tar was speaking the truth about Sae in that moment. He had not chosen his Akuan brothers over Sae because he had loved his brothers so. That was a lie he had told himself at the time and desperately wanted to believe.

No, he had stayed with the Akuan for one simple reason. Because Tar knew Quinn's past as the Nameless Man. A past that Quinn had forgotten and wished to reclaim above all else. Quinn could lie to himself but not to an outside observer, a mind reader like Tar.

"It's as I said, Quinny . . . All we have left are questions . . . Why'd you involve yourself with that dangerous woman? Why did I let you? How can we lie to the rest of the Akuan about our true mutant natures, then kill others of our kind without any regrets or remorse? Why did I have you kill Telligood and not Sae for being a Rogue Caster?

"What really is the Void? What is the Forbidden One's real purpose in our human world? Is the alien organism that has taken possession of this ancient forest the Forbidden One? Is this its final form?"

At Tar's words, Quinn looked around at the rough, alien skin that grew over the dark soil they sat upon. He shook his head, not wanting to imagine the horror at the center of where it all came from. Tar continued, his eyes transfixed by the dwindling embers of the campfire.

"What shall I do now to slay it? How shall I go on without my brothers? Who is the man I was before? Shall I be that man again? Questions, Quinny, so many questions. It's the only thing we have an abundance of now. How we deal with the unknowns that come with serious questions like those determines what and who we are. My friend, my brother... I ask you only one question, the most important one I could ever ask. Do you still trust me?"

Quinn looked down at his muddy boots, away from Tar's pleading eyes. As his heated anger waned further, his tears flowed.

"Yes, I do, sir."

"Then these questions should not matter to you in this peaceful moment. Let go, my friend, of your need to know your terrible past. Trust me when I say to you that only pain and suffering would have awaited you upon hearing the truths I would have revealed."

"Should I have run away with her? Should I have just left you all and tried to blunt myself into something other than a blade by Sae's side?"

"That's another question I don't know the answer to. All I know, my friend, my brother, is you trust me, I trust you. That is all that remains to fill the void in our souls that our brothers' lives once collectively filled. You and I have lost our entire Akuan family in the span of one campaign.

"We are all each other has left in this world. And soon, my friend, you'll be back to where you started from. All alone." Tar grinned with sadness and pain. Quinn looked away from his mentor's pale face, his heart gripped in a painful chokehold that filled every waking moment.

"Sir . . . My friend. It sounds like you've just given up on hope."

Tar smiled as he watched the fire finally go out beside them. The small iron cup they had used for boiling water still glowed bright red, even though the fire did not.

"I'm your Akuan Commander, Quinny. I cannot afford the luxury of giving up."

A few quiet moments later, after a pause that even the wild denizens of the Deep Woods unknowingly observed, Quinn realized he cradled not a dying man but a dead one. He was as he had feared from the beginning. Alone.

His mind, realizing that his worst fear had just been realized, forced him to cry out in agony. His heart beat hard thumps. His tired eyes flowed heavily with tears.

In that moment the Nameless Man, the now brotherless and friendless being, bit into his own selfish streak. Quinn didn't weep for Tar, nor for his lost brothers. Not wholly. Instead, he wept first and foremost for himself.

For the last light of life had just gone out for the Akuan, and with it, the purpose for his struggle, his existence. For everyone everywhere knows that there cannot be a sole survivor of an Akuan. In the same way that a lone individual can never call themselves a family, a lone Akuansman can never call himself a one-man Akuan.

In the moment that Tar died by a wound he didn't care to show until the very end, the Silver Serpent Akuan died as a whole, just like its former members. Quinn was no longer a probationary Silver Serpent, no longer an Akuansman in the making. He was just a Rogue Caster on the run. His self-identity laid to waste, the key to recovering his past self was now also forever gone.

Or so the many voices of despair in his mind told him. Quinn, following Tar's last order, just sat and listened to the sound of nothingness. To the voice of his mentor that was no longer there. He wallowed in the den of despair, regret, and heartache like he was a permanent resident there. That is, until he heard a sound like nothing else. A sound he was not expecting.

"What's this nonsense? Stiff upper lip, lad."

Shocked to hear a human voice, Quinn looked up to see Fredstar, his senior second adjunct.

"Remember the First Oath. Strike first and strike fast. You must seize back the initiative from this fiend and pull yourself together!" The dark-skinned, gray-haired man who was a sergeant most of his life looked down at Quinn from beyond the iron cup's glowing light with a steadfast grin.

Quinn relaxed from his shock as he realized that Fredstar wasn't really there. It was just a lingering memory of the old man who had died to the first Herald.

"Look at 'em. Things go to shit, and he falls to pieces. Quinn, you really got some learnin' left to do," said Michael, appearing next to Fredstar with a smile, seemingly out of thin air.

"Aye, Quinn. Get this bloody fire goin' again. It's your job to see to this mundane bullshit. You're on probation after all, mate." Quinn looked away from Fredstar and Michael to Tryan, who was now sitting casually in front of the fire opposite from where Quinn still cradled Tar's corpse in his arms. Tryan the jokester grinned at Quinn. Yet another memory had come alive.

"Cynicism is counterfeit wisdom. Cynicism is the death of truth. You must stop your reckless cynicism about this world and trust the good we see in you," said Bryon the hulking giant as Quinn turned his head to see him walk by from behind him, then sit at the campfire next to his nonidentical twin brother.

"Stop pretending to be smart Bryon. You ain't," said Tryan, slightly annoyed.

Bryon looked at his brother with a dumb expression, then said, "I'm dead. What better time to reinvent myself, right?" Bryon then looked at Quinn with a smirk.

"Remember, Quinn . . . A peace up here." The redheaded Red came out of the black of the night toward the campfire, pointing to his head. "Is greater than a peace out there." Red then pointed in the direction of the center of the Deep Woods.

"Oh, look who's finally showed up. Red, where 'ave you been? I was looking for you in the afterlife. Wasn't sure you'd show," Bryon said as Red sat beside him. The cheeky grin on Red's face at Bryon's question told everyone he had quite an interesting tale about why he was so late to die.

"The wages of sin is death. They should have tossed you into hell, Red," Seppa said dramatically while inspecting the head of an arrow as he leaned against a nearby tree. He appeared from nowhere as yet another strange figure from Quinn's memories, amalgamated with living imagination. In other words, he appeared as a ghost from Quinn's past.

"Off ya high horse, Seppa. I'm not that bad," Red said with a relaxed grin.

"You do evil in this world, and the world shall pay you back in kind. For evil does not like the company of other evils, for it is a threat to itself. Perhaps that's why Red was kicked out of hell," the bearded Samson said as he sat at the dwindled campfire among his other seated brothers. He flashed a charismatic smile that infectiously spread among the men as they laughed at his lighthearted joke.

Quinn had admired Samson. He always nurtured good nature in the hearts of his subordinates, even in death. The role of first adjunct was one he was born to be, and he died playing it proudly.

Quinn, thinking himself crazier by the moment from what he could see playing out before him, looked around at his brothers' faces, not knowing what to think anymore. They all looked so real, and yet he knew they weren't. Were they ghosts? Ethereal beings that came to bless their last remaining living battle brother before moving to another plane of existence?

No, that is not how the logical, always-serious-about-everything man named Quinn saw it. Upon great reflection later, he saw in this happening a delusion of his exhausted mind paired with subconscious thought. Something like a waking dream gone mad. But perhaps he was wrong. Perhaps there was something else in this happening that he didn't have the open mind to see.

"You are all dead! You can't be here . . ." Quinn finally said through tears.

"And yet, Quinny . . . We all are," Tar said as he too appeared at the campfire, igniting the fire into a vivid blaze as soon as he came close. Quinn looked from Tar's grinning face to the Tar in his arms who smiled no more. He shook his head in despair. He thought he had finally gone insane.

"You can either be overwhelmed with all the good in this world or the bad. It's your choice. I know that now," said Red, likely reflecting on the manner of his own death as he stared at the campfire.

"The end is in sight for you now. I must admit I am slightly jealous you shall pull off this impossible feat all alone. My, the glory you shall earn. Enough to build a legend for sure," said Seppa as he too stared distantly at the campfire, which flicked light into everyone's familiar faces.

"Don't get jealous, Seppa. He has his burdens as we all do. Now, I fear we are taking too much of our brother's precious time. Quinn has better things to do than talk to the dead. Say your final piece to brother Quinn, lads. It's time for us to move on, forever." Samson got up from the fireside, then said with a genuine smile, "I hope you understand what I mean when I say we don't want to see you anytime soon." Samson then turned and disappeared from sight.

"You are not alone," said Fredstar before he too disappeared into the darkness.

"You never were," said Seppa as he leaned off the tree, then departed from existence.

"We will all live on in you, mate," said Red as he too left our material realm.

"So go do it. Carry us across the line," said Bryon as he got up and walked past Quinn into complete nothingness.

"Make our deaths mean something. I didn't sacrifice myself for some bullshit. I died so you could keep kicking Voidling arse, that's what." Tryan got up with a smile then disappeared from this life as well.

"You'll be alright, mate. Worst case, you'll just end up where we are," said Michael as he too left forever. Leaving only Quinn, Tar's corpse, and the strange specter of Tar in front of him. They sat around the still blazing fire together like the strangest trio in history.

"Quinny, I'm sorry I couldn't tell you what you wanted to know. But as way of apology, I shall tell you now in death what you need to know to go on," Tar said with a smile from across the burning-bright campfire. Quinn was having none of it though. He had no time for imagined words from beyond the grave.

"You all say you are still a part of me! Still alive within me now. Yet I feel so hollow inside. Is this not just my deluded mind telling me what I wish to hear?" Quinn shook his head in anguish as the specter of Tar said nothing.

"How can I go on without you all? You all were my reason to be, and yet I did not realize that until now, now that you are forever gone." Quinn cried out to the specter in front of him, still unsure whether or not he was just talking to himself.

"We became your reason for being in life; we can become your reason for being in death. Almost nothing has changed. Has it, Quinny? Don't you realize that with our untimely deaths, it means the Forbidden One no longer has any leverage against you. You no longer have anything to lose. It can't kill what is already dead.

"Yet as every one of your brothers has said, we live on now in a form that the Forbidden One can never remove. From this moment on, Quinny, you will never be alone. For in death, we can always reside within you. Etched into your heart, your history, your living thoughts . . . Forever."

"Except if I forget again, just as I did with my past. If I can forget my own name, I'll for sure forget yours," Quinn said angrily, to which Tar just smiled, easily dismissing his thought.

"You'll eventually remember us again should the worst happen. Of that I have no doubt. Just as I believe you will remember the man you were before if you give yourself long enough."

Quinn, not wishing to accept this answer, shook his head in disbelief. The word of this unknown specter could not sway him even though its logic was sound. The emotions he felt, his feelings of despair, were simply too strong. They washed out all reason from his ears. They made the truth into a dark fallacy in which everything was the color of death.

The specter of Tar must have seen this as he then said, "Quinny, know that fear is not a logical beast. You cannot reason with it or out of it. Do not let it guide you forthwith. For if it does, laddie . . ."

Quinn shook his head as he spoke to madness.

"I know, Tar, I know. It'll destroy whatever chance is left to kill the fiend. If I give into fear now, the being that killed you all wins," Quinn said as his heart bled out.

"Know, my brother, that a part of me will always go with you. Remember the Fifth Oath. It may save your life one day. Quinny, my heart breaks for you. Yet, I cannot help you any more than this or tell you what is to happen after I depart. But know this, there will be a choice at the end of this journey. One you will not wish to make." Quinn looked up at the specter, at the serious green-eyed stare of his mentor, which would sometimes mirror his own.

"I ask that when you choose between the two bad options presented, you will choose the one that will cause you the most pain."

"What are you talking about?" Quinn said dismissively. Tar's specter stood up then came to crouch next to Quinn and its own corpse.

"I can't explain that now. There is no more time. Choose pain over what feels good in the moment, my friend, for that is the path of righteousness."

"I still don't understand!" Quinn said, shaking his head. Specter Tar forced his concern into a smile, then stood up, looking down at the man who had been made a sobbing child by fear and doubt, cowering in front of him.

With a growing look of pride that seemed inappropriate at the moment, Tar said, "Life consists of moments like this, moments of fleeting ostentation. Richly felt moments in life both good and bad. Seize them, each and every one. Now go! Show the world that even fakes like us can be true heroes."

Before Quinn's eyes, Tar disappeared. Not the corpse he held but the version of the man that had seemingly come back to life as a specter, a ghost of the dead. Quinn looked around. Even his own delusions had abandoned him, or so he thought. Feeling alone, despite what was said, he cried.

"My brothers, you left too soon. What shall I do now without you all? I do not wish to suffer through life alone."

Quinn slumped over Tar's corpse. His hands shaking, his heart broken beyond repair. Like a fetus in the womb, he held himself tightly and made himself small. A long while passed with him like this in utter, prolonged silence. Nothing felt right, and nothing felt like it would ever change to be otherwise. But like all things, his sadness, his mourning had to eventually come to an end.

A great wind interrupted the quiet moment, coming into the scene as quick as the speed of sound. Upon said wind, Quinn heard all the voices of the brothers he had lost as one. Laid over and into another, they said, "To the young girl's coffin, the one that we buried, dig it up. Bring it before the Forbidden One. Take its life like it took ours. There can be no forgiveness, no mercy. You are the judgment of the dead, Quinn, our executioner's blade in human form."

The breeze left, and with it the voices of the men he had loved. Following Tar's last words, Quinn had listened for an order for hours while in despondency, and he finally heard one. Whether imagined or not, he no longer cared. For he now had a way to be an Akuansman, a warrior pitted against the Void again. A way to stop being useless and to cry no longer.

Judgment. He could become the hand of judgment from out of the grave. Yes, he thought—yes! Perhaps the fire of vengeance would be enough to ignite his will to live on, to fight on and win yet again enduring all hardships.

Revenge, justice by its other name. To wrong those that wronged you, the most innate desire we humans have . . . Yes! What he found within himself was drive enough to move forward. His hatred would give the Forbidden One's death a greater meaning than leaving it merely a cold corpse. That would be worthy of the excruciating, all-encompassing effort that almost certainly would be required to do in the alien foe.

Quinn, having lost the will to be a sad, miserable man in that moment, decided to be reborn with the morning's first light. He rose from his despair with the twinkling of sunrays upon him. The corpse of Tar laid gently aside; he was no longer human in his eyes. He breathed, he sweated, he groaned one thing only. Yes, vengeance. That was his new identity.

As his eyes dried with the growing heat of day and his face turned from mourning into stone, he decided that he was the self-anointed judgment of mankind against the Forbidden One . . . The amalgamation of both hate and righteousness incarnate. If there could be no others, if all other humans within the Forbidden One's new domain were now slain, it would have to be him alone.

On the eleventh day of the campaign against the Forbidden One, Quinn, who had been called many different names throughout history, hence the title of the Nameless Man, for no name has ever stuck upon him, named himself Justice, for the dead.

Chapter 10 – The Roar of Life

Quinn sprinted through the lands called the Deep Woods. He was horrified by the alien sights, smells, and sounds all around him. The once-fertile ancient forest was now wholly beset and assaulted by the alien organism that consumed it with the gusto of a flesh-eating disease.

It became clear as Quinn leaped, with each step supernaturally strengthened by his Gift powers, that at the center of all this chaos would no longer be a forest of any kind but a wasteland of alien origin. A place of high heat and humidity wherein the trees "melted" into running streams of viscous black goo, the horrifying beginnings of which he could see all around him.

Bells! Quinn thought as he ran through this hellscape and the sun beat down heavily upon his sweaty brow. *Bells, what kind of monster shall I find there?* he thought as he kept running, kept charging forth, knowing that this could be his last hurrah as Quinn. For while he was immortal and removed from permanent death, he knew from recent experience that there are worse things in life than dying horribly. Having to be reborn in a hostile world all alone, ignorant of your true identity was one of them.

Quinn, with the ethos of a marathon runner, ran through heat waves that would have seen a normal, unmutated man boil with heatstroke. As the forest around him slowly transformed into pools of black pus and alien bile that would then be absorbed by the alien skin underneath, Quinn persevered, having finally found a reason good enough to risk what little the Forbidden One had not stolen from him yet. Vengeance would be his.

Seemingly unaffected by the immense heat bearing down, three foes of the Void leaped from concealment behind the slowly "melting" forest undergrowth. Three Zardlions, a type of Void beast that looks like a small, bony fox.

Normally a creature of total darkness that scavenges from the felled prey of larger Voidlings, the seemingly enraged Zardlions attacked Quinn as soon as they saw him. Their razor-sharp jaws pitted against his bare hands. It was no contest. Quinn, barely breaking his stride, smashed through the three bony exoskeleton foxes with his bare knuckles.

Punching one of their heads into oblivion as it leapt at him, then supernaturally quick, he grabbed the other two by their necks mid-flight and slammed them into the hard, alien-skinned ground below. Snapping every bone in their body in the process, making them but sacks of flesh unable to move, only whimper. Such was Quinn's resounding superhuman strength when elevated by his Gift power.

He ran on for hours that morning of the eleventh day. Land that took him and his brothers hours to traverse more than a week ago took minutes. The alien organism had inadvertently eaten a pathway through the undergrowth and other natural barriers previously blocking easy travel.

The Forbidden One, somehow sensing Quinn was hastily approaching, fearful of the incoming threat that was our man of judgment, started to scrape the bottom of its otherworldly barrel of horrors. It sent everything, absolutely everything it had at Quinn front on.

Like with the Zardlions, Quinn tore through all these fiends with bare hands, blunt sword, and dagger. With the voracity of a madman, he had no patience for them. It is not a stretch to say that Quinn went a little mad.

But then again, to become a worthy adversary of the Void, one must first be a little mad, a little crazy. However, his battle frenzy did not dispel his ability to think and reason clearly. For it was as he ran, slew, ran some more, and slew some more that he realized a truth. A truth like that which Pell's tall tale had foretold him to seek.

Yes, the final part of Pell's tale had finally come true. Quinn had realized the hidden truth of the Deep Woods. The truth the Forbidden One did not wish Quinn to speak. Quinn found it buried there in his various painful yet hopeful memories of the past. Those made during the likes of this disastrous campaign.

You see, as he ran, he finally had time to think. He used that time to stop looking back at all the strange happenings during this campaign as randomness and consider each in singular depth. He considered the fact that a magical-sounding, alleged curse, cast by a Voidling of all things, was placed and triggered upon the residents of Parika' Te Mo. A thing without precedent found nowhere else in life but in fairy tales.

He considered again the appearances of the strange sentient Heralds, which Tar supernaturally sensed both existed and didn't exist at the same time. He then pondered the one-by-one manner of his brothers' deaths and his "vision" from the afterlife shortly after they all died. Bells! He lamented again that an ungifted old fart from a town in the middle of nowhere foresaw it all in his tall tale—everything! It didn't make sense!

Until Quinn reminded himself that everything, absolutely everything, happens for a reason. Even those of the Void must be governed by the laws of cause and effect. If not in their own realm, at least in ours. As soon as Quinn considered these events as not being of a chaotic Void-like nature but as one series of logical, planned, and well-thought-out happenings, a new frightening idea developed in his mind. Something that not even the wise Tar had considered.

It was as he made this realization concerning the real truth of the Deep Woods that he came across the place of pain he was searching for. He ran into a clearing where three lonely graves were laid out. Still covered in the shade of nearby melting trees, Quinn found the graves of Debbie's daughter; Fredstar, his senior second adjunct; and the formerly possessed child laid left to right in a row.

Quinn didn't hesitate as he rushed over to the grave that hid Debbie's daughter's coffined corpse. He was glad that the graves were dug shallow, as the forest had too many roots for a deep burial. Quinn now realized, after ripping off the grave's burial stones with abandon, that he never bothered to learn this little dead girl's name, yet now everything relied upon her.

Once the burial stones were cast away, Quinn clawed with his hands, braking fingernails and scraping his hands raw in an effort to dig into the grave and uncover the coffin below as quickly as possible. Sensing he could be attacked at any moment now that his back was turned, he dug past the layer of alien skin that wished to encroach upon all.

It was fortunate for him that the alien organism was simply covering the earth, not growing itself into the ground like a tree with roots. This meant that when Quinn finally came to the rotten, still-swampy wooden coffin underneath the black topsoil, it was highly unlikely the alien organism would have consumed the little girl's corpse within. The very key to unlocking and overcoming everything that was going on was, once again, the dead body of a nameless child who drowned in a well.

Quinn, using his supernatural strength, easily tore the coffin from its resting place in the shallow grave. It was half out of the grave when Quinn felt peering eyes upon him.

Quinn stepped out of the shallow grave, the rotting wooden coffin slanted to the side. He looked around at the many, many shadowy figures that were revealing themselves in increasingly great number by the second. Ten, twenty, no, thirty? No, at least forty it was. Perhaps even more.

He looked at them all with hate on his sweaty expression, at the humanoid shapes that emerged from the melting forest's darkness and into the boiling light of the sun. It was when Quinn saw them for what they were in the daylight that his suspicions surrounding the Deep Woods mystery were confirmed as not theory but as undeniable fact.

The scent of death was strong on the old man's bellow as tribalistic, Void-afflicted men and women stood all around him in plain view. Wielding clubs, bone knifes, and barely functional bows, these wild-eyed, gray-skinned humans who acted like Voidlings, looked at Quinn through the torn eyeholes of skinned flesh from other people's faces.

"Face-Stealers . . . I hate Face-Stealers!" Quinn spat with rage as he said aloud his most hated foe's name. The Face-Stealers of Danneish, the wild madman cult of cannibal people, had come close to killing and consuming him once before. That dark near-death experience had festered with time and resulted in a biting hatred of them ever since.

In that moment, as Quinn was surrounded by his most loathed enemy, the next and final foe appeared. It came onto the scene as a disembodied voice.

"I've been waiting . . ." said the voice of a pleasant, feminine, and reasonable-sounding young woman. The words came into Quinn's mind without need for his ears. He recognized it as an act of telepathy straight away. If it was really the Forbidden One, it sounded nothing like he thought it might. Disturbingly, it sounded more human than anything.

"Who are you? Voice in my head?" he said aloud as his eyes searched the motionless Face-Stealers all around him, readying themselves for a telepathic attack order that might come at any moment.

"Who am I, you ask? The simplest explanation is that I am the one who destroyed Parika' Te Mo. I'm the one who made your brothers die hopelessly before you. I am Del'more Kar'dia. The Forbidden One is what you call me, yes. Quinn, I am the Voidling you've come to slay." Quinn grimaced at the being's unapologetic words. Seeing this, the being taunted.

"Say my name, Rogue Caster. I dare you to say it aloud. For if you do, your life will become mine. Just like these mindless Void-touched servants before you."

Quinn, unafraid of the Forbidden One, yelled at the top of his lungs, "DEL'MORE KAR'DIA!" The melting forest stood in silent shock for a moment. And then—nothing happened. Quinn, realizing he still possessed his perfect faculties, grinned from ear to ear. He called her bluff.

"Again, Forbidden One, you lean into a made-up story by a crazy old coot of a man. As I suspected, you showed us not what you truly were but what we expected to see. The Rellian that Tar was searching for in the form of a child, which Bryon was searching for. Then when we returned to the town which you destroyed, what happened? Michael found the foe, the Toothy Spider he was searching for. As did Seppa when he was snatched away before us by that headless bird. Bells, I know the truth now!" Quinn spat as he talked with rage boiling within him.

"They were all made-up! Weren't they?!"

"I don't know of what you speak, human."

"Yes, you do! Don't give me that! The truth of the Deep Woods is that it both exists and doesn't exist at the same time. With your appearance here using powers beyond human understanding, you have transformed this domain into a realm of pure thought and imagination! You can wish anything into existence here. So long as we humans think of it first."

"Your mind is playing tricks on you, mortal. You are wrong."

"Don't pretend to think me mortal either! We both know I cannot die. Answer me, Voidling. Admit to me the truth before I put you and your servants to the sword. Did you make up my brethren's deaths just as you did the Heralds themselves?"

"I don't know of what you spe—"

"YES, YOU DO!" Quinn roared, interrupting the Forbidden One's voice in his head. "Look at these foul, corrupted humans around me. There are no Face-Stealer tribes in these parts. Tar was right! If they actually lived here, they would have all been eaten as Voidlings like to hunt them as well as us. Yet Seppa, when I was last here, saw their fake shadows. His fearful mind imagined something, and you brought it into existence here before me.

"You have used our imaginations, our deep-seated fears against us from the very start of this campaign we waged against you. Now I realize it all wasn't initially real. Our hopelessness and fear enabled you to kill us with monsters from our own thoughts."

Del'more Kar'dia laughed out loud in a girlish, mocking tone before finally speaking through use of telepathy.

"Let's test your theory, mortal. Let's test just how real these twisted humans before you be," the young woman said as she snickered meanly.

As soon as her voice departed from his mind, the Face-Stealers roared an animalistic chant of madness-induced rage. Quinn, accepting the challenge, let out what could only be described as the roar of life itself.

For he battled in that moment not against the Forbidden One, not against what was real or not, but in his own heart, against death itself. Against everything that accosted and regaled him harshly: the facts of our fleeting lives, the shadow of death itself that hangs heavily over us all, even when our chins are lifted high. Quinn fought physically in that moment but also spiritually and poetically in that he labored to reclaim life in the midst of darkness and death.

Humanity. Life. The Void. Death. Each had chosen its champion that day, and the hand of fate chose Quinn to be our representative. Our blade. For none other than Quinn could have sustained such an action on that dark day. No man other than Quinn could become our judgment incarnate.

He swung around and picked up Fredstar's still-sharp sword, which had formerly stuck out of Fredstar's grave in

131

remembrance. The Face-Stealers all piled onto Quinn in great number, but Quinn, grasping Fredstar's blade, the blade of the man who was known as the iron will of the Silver Serpents, cut through the mass of bodies with pure, unadulterated fury.

Yet even after the first row of their screaming ranks were eviscerated, sliced to hundreds of meaty pieces, the second row amassed on him in their place without a single moment's hesitation. Over forty of their cannibal tribe, who were driven completely mad by ongoing proximity to Void tears, rushed in like a human tidal wave of raggedly clothed, gray-skinned bodies.

Some Face-Stealers held back in the trees as the rest charged. From there, they loosed arrow after arrow into Quinn as he fought against foes on all sides until his back, torso, and legs were pierced many times over by arrows with feathered plumes, making him look like a human pincushion. And yet he fought on!

If that wasn't enough, they beat at his flesh with stone axes and blunt clubs as they overwhelmed his defenses not by skill but by superior numbers. Some even got close enough to grab him with their defiled hands, which were still soaked in the dried blood of animals and humans alike.

In the process of trying to pin him down, the Face-Stealers ripped off Quinn's dark green Silver Serpent cloak, tearing it into tatters, as well as the under armor beneath it. The violent act exposed his now bloody and bruised chest to the elements as he thrashed against the many hands laboring to pull him to his death, to the alien-skinned ground below. Quinn was quickly being overcome by the tide of bodies around him.

Despite this, Quinn fought on like a berserker, a mindless enraged barbarian. Despite them all, he broke free of the animalistic onslaught, and with his superhuman strength, he slowly began to take back the initiative. His muscles flexed at every cleave of his sword, every blow that saw an explosion of gore and brain matter from the smashing of cannibal skulls. Quinn, alone, fought on.

Quinn bled out rivers of blood from his arrow wounds and the numerous stab marks all along his body and even his head. Despite all this, Quinn acted like the unstoppable force of nature that he was. For every wound inflicted on him, he simply channeled his inner warmth and completely healed himself of the blow within a moment. This was his most powerful asset of war, his personal healing Gift.

This is why they called the Nameless Man a killing machine. A blade that cannot ever be blunted! For as the waves of human bodies crashed against the shore that was the weapon called Quinn, eventually the impossible happened. The sea gave in.

Quinn snapped the neck of the last Face-Stealer within arm's reach, dropping the smaller man onto the pile of disfigured corpses at his feet. Quinn looked at the Face-Stealers who were still alive only because they had kept their distance. Only the archers remained of their previously large number. He gave them a look of utter menace, evil and twisted enough that even a Void-afflicted madman was driven to flight by the sight of it. The Face-Stealers ran from their judgment, as all weak men like them do.

Quinn, now safe for the moment, looked around at what had become a mass graveyard. As he started to painfully pull arrows from his body, and as his cuts and bruises slowly started to heal en masse, he saw in the flash of a moment Tar's tired, dying face.

"We are both killing machines, Quinn," he heard old Tar say.

In that moment, if not for his immense rage, he would have cried out aloud. For Quinn, the Nameless Man, had always hated what he was, yet whether by fate or curse, he could never be anything but a human-shaped blade.

"Beautiful . . . What a work of art you've painted all around you. Ha . . . And you call me a monster," said Del'more Kar'dia.

"Shut your mouth!"

133

"Shut yours! Don't you know there is nowhere as peaceful as a graveyard? Enjoy your newfound peace while you can," she said wickedly, singularly enjoying the sound of her own joke.

Quinn, having removed all the arrows from his body, flicked Fredstar's still-sharp blade clean. The blood dripping from Quinn in rivers was no longer his own. His hair was now red. His chest was now red. His legs, his pants, all red. His boots sloshed with so much blood that he kicked them off and went onward barefoot.

The heat, which had not relented, would soon dry off the sticky blood of his enemies, he thought as he walked forward toward the shallow grave.

"I like you, Quinn. I could have ended you by now, you do realize. But I haven't. I've singled you out. I bothered to know your name. What reason do you fathom, human, that I have gone this far for you?"

"You fear me," Quinn said as he dragged the coffin out of the grave now pooling with blood. "You wish to understand what you fear in hopes you may overcome me. Yet, you now know me. You've watched all that I did and didn't do. All I said and didn't say." Quinn, using the rope straps still on the coffin from when he and his brothers carried it there, hefted the coffin onto his back.

He wore it as a backpack of sorts; the small child's coffin would prevent him from running but not much else. He continued speaking to the voice in his head, this time with a deep, roaring tone in his breath.

"I bet you've learned more about me than you wished to know through the course of this campaign my brothers and I waged against you. And yet, I can tell from the fact you hide from me even now that you fear me still. To fear the unknown is one thing; to fear the known quantity is something else. Something much worse. I fear you less than you fear me, Del'more Kar'dia."

"I actually agree, mortal. In fact, if this was a child's or simpleton's tale, you'd probably be the villain here. Not little old me."

"And that makes you what? The hero?" Quinn said as he continued his trek north, away from the bloody graveyard he almost singularly planted in the earth. The alien skin was already absorbing the corpses, he observed in disgust.

"I'm the hero of my story. You're the hero of yours. We all get to be heroes, Quinn. That's what makes existence interesting."

"STOP WASTING MY TIME! Tell me! Where are my brothers?! The fact your—" Quinn's words of rage were cut off mid-sentence, for out of the shadow of a melting stoa oak as old as thirteen centuries, two familiar faces joined his company.

"Gus . . . Lichale . . ." Quinn said with horror as he saw the two Silver Serpent brothers yet to be accounted for. The ones who Tar and he had waited for by a dwindling campfire until past midnight yet never reunited with.

Where there once was life on their faces there was now a pale sense of undeath. Their jaws were stretched unnaturally long with fanged teeth. Their strides were that of deranged men who could barely walk in a straight line as they twitched uncontrollably with every step. Their hands had fallen away from their wrists, and bony white claws grew in their place.

They had both died and become Biters. The disease that turned them into such upon death had afflicted them as it does one in five members of humanity. Had Quinn known he would have to see them like this, he would have never wished to be reunited with them. Knowing this, Del'more Kar'dia laughed as both mindless Biters, driven only by endless hunger, rushed Quinn with their newly found fangs and claws.

Quinn, with tears in his eyes, easily dispatched them with but two simple flicks of Fredstar's sword. The men he used to know fell motionless by his bare feet, and with great pain and

135

reluctance, he stabbed each in the heart. Making sure that they would truly enjoy an eternal peace.

"See, mortal, how generous I am to you? I let you say goodbye to your last remaining family, your friends. You should thank me. Better yet, you should love me! For I am evil and twisted in the same ways as you."

"Who are you? Bride of death. Of misfortune as well, to say you know me?" said Quinn as his logical mind labored heavily to move his heartbroken body forward.

"Who am I? Who are you? Isn't that the real question here? Should I endure advice about identity from a man who doesn't even know his own?"

"I am the hope of my brothers lost. I am the judgment of the dead. That is who I am," Quinn said, steeling himself against the words of the enemy.

"How boring . . ." said the young woman's unescapable voice in Quinn's head. "You'd think you'd have better things to do than get revenge for the dead. Tell me, mortal, why try so hard for people who no longer exist?"

"Oh, they exist.' Quinn gripped Fredstar's blade tightly as he moved the coffin's strap higher over his shoulder. "If they exist no longer in this realm, then the only place they remain is within me."

Quinn marched onward with Fredstar's sword in one hand and the ropes of the coffin in the other. Quinn proceeded deeper into the Deep Woods, albeit at a much slower pace than before.

As he faced the blistered, dark alien forest in front of him, its high trees melting moment by moment, he saw many shining Voidling eyes peering back at him from the darkness. He knew in that moment that the "easy" part was over. There was nothing left to do but finally slay the Forbidden One.

***

136

"You know, Quinn, Quinny, that pain you feel inside always? That one you wear not on your face but on your heart every waking moment of every day and restless, tired night? The thing that has recently increased its torture of you like never before because of your battle brothers' recent untimely deaths? You know it's all just chemicals, right? Toxins mixing in your brain. Sadness is but a chemical formula for you humans, as is joy. It's all made-up, what you feel, mortal. If you'd let me, I could help," said Del'more Kar'dia in a compassionate-sounding tone.

"What I feel now is not made-up!" Quinn roared aloud as he smashed in the head of a Screamer, a large two-legged lizard with a frilled neck and razor-sharp fangs. Standing half the size of a man, it and its five brethren were no match for one enraged Quinn. "There is no drug that could take away the pain of my loss!"

"Oh, but there is. You just haven't looked hard enough."

"I believe nothing you say, Del'more Kar'dia. How can a wicked Voidling like you understand the depths of humanity?"

"Ha! I've observed you human creatures much in the short one hundred years I've been here in your realm. You lot do not operate according to principles of high logic or superior morality. You are hedonistic, going and doing whatever produces the most pleasure-inducing chemicals in your brains. I could induce such a euphoric bliss in your mind that you'd never know sadness or loss or loneliness ever again. You only need to wish it."

Quinn continued forward, facing an onslaught of Voidlings against him at every step as he slowly got closer to the center of the Deep Woods. Tooth, claw, tentacle. It was all the same to him at this point. He cared not but for the kill that really mattered. He at first thought that this verbal joust between the Forbidden One and him was meaningless. However, now he realized it was simply another means of warfare at his disposal.

137

"The meaning of life goes beyond a dopamine hit in the brain. It is greater than the pleasures of the flesh," Quinn said as a Fltior swiped its webbed hand across Quinn's face, drawing much blood. In retaliation, Quinn swiped it back with Fredstar's now-blunt sword, cleaving the Voidling in two by sheer force alone. He then continued his pointed words.

"The meaning of life to me is to fight against the shadow of death. To create life and meaning where previously there was none. We humans are creators; that is our purpose. As for you, I know you to be a destroyer. A consumer of our world, and so as a creator of life, I cannot live in peace with you."

Del'more Kar'dia saw she had no ground she could take from Quinn in this area, and so like with many of the debates they had for the past few hours, she stopped talking. Then she moved onto the next potential weak link in Quinn's mental armor.

"Tar lied to you, you know. Lied to your brothers. And I'm not just speaking of him hiding his Rogue Caster identity either. He proclaimed a false hope that even he knew would never eventuate. I mean, look at you now, all alone; he effectively promised everyone they'd make it if they believed they would. Yet they didn't. He lied to those he loved. To you. Why claim vengeance for a man like that?"

"It is true, Tar knew that he and the rest of my brothers would likely be killed in our second attempt to get here."

"He lied! He made up hope where there was no hope to be had," Del'more Kar'dia said in a pushy tone.

"No, he didn't. I realize now that his hope wasn't in the Akuan making it but in me alone. I am the hope of my brothers now. Tar committed his entire Akuan, his life's work and that of the family he loved, to the labor of slaying you. He was convinced you needed to die. In this thought, I am with him. For I have never heard of a Voidling like you before, and after seeing what you've done, I am convinced a being like you should not exist!"

Del'more again and again continued to fail in swaying away Quinn from his path of vengeance. Step by step, he was inching closer to her. No doubt, she could feel every step.

"So then, you will not be frightened away. I can accept that. Maybe. What if I make a way clear for you to escape? I give you an easier option than having to kill me. What if I temporarily lift my curse upon these lands? I'll let you run. Help you even, if you promise to never return. Surely you wish to be somewhere else, any other place than here. I can promise you that not a single Voidling shall try and stop you from leaving, if you agree to my terms."

"Never!" said Quinn as he stepped down upon the neck of yet another Voidling beast, driving the sword through its singular eyehole as its carapace could deflect all steel arrayed against it. "All that I have left in this world is in this swamp! This fakkin' forest of the dammed! No price, no threat, could make me flee you," Quinn roared.

"Oh really?" the Forbidden One said in Quinn's head, seemingly knowing better than him about this. "I know what you are really trying to do here. As you walk toward me with that child's coffin on your back, swaying with every swing of your sword. You are imagining a reality in which I can bring your brothers back from the dead. Normally, it wouldn't be possible, but by use of the curse here . . . You think, just perhaps, it will be enough."

"And I know what you are doing also. You keep calling me mortal in the hope that I will imagine myself as such and then you'll be able to kill me. Permanently. It shall not work," Quinn said with absolute resolve.

"You really have gone mad. You are nothing but an eloquent barbarian. They are all dead! Tar, Gus, Lichale, the two twins with confusing names. BELLS! Get it into your thick human skull! They are dead! Never ever to return to this realm."

"Why don't I believe you?" Quinn growled.

"Because you hang onto a foolish hope, you idiot! Why even go on, mortal? You'll win here for what? The dead? They do not care for such things. Nobody will know what you did here. Even less than nobody will care."

"I care."

"Exactly my point. You are less than a nobody. You are an outcast among outcasts of your race. What is your hope in? Do you really wish to one day grow old and die in your sleep like other men of your race? Bells, it seems like I can save you from that boring fate and end all your troubles by ending you here and now. How about you let me give you your own eternal rest?"

"No. I look forward to growing old and wise like Tar. And as for my death . . . should I ever be able to truly die. The way I see it, death is as natural for us humans as birth. I am not frightened by it. You don't know this because you've never done it before, Voidling. But dying is boring and easy. Living is the hard, interesting part," Quinn said as he slayed the last of his animalistic Voidling foes and came toward what seemed to be a wide-open clearing gleaming in the hot sun.

"Ha . . . You know what I think, mortal? I think you consider yourself strong because, unconsciously, you already know you are dead inside. You act in defiance of me only because you believe I can no longer hurt you more than I already have. That idea is blatantly false."

"A blade feels no pain when it cuts," a tired Quinn said as he dragged Fredstar's cold, bloody blade by his side. The straps holding the child's coffin to him rubbed his flesh raw moment by moment. After five long hours of constant physical and mental battles and having slept not a single wink the night before, Quinn was tired. Exhausted like never before.

"Yet you are not a blade. For you feel a deep-seated pain within yourself every day. It's the reason why you won't end up winning against me," Del'more said sternly.

140

Quinn smirked as he dragged himself into the large clearing, to a pool at the very center of the Deep Woods, which could now be called the Deep Lakes instead. As he trekked near the center of the alien organism that was consuming all the lifeforce from nearby lands with its otherworldly presence, he threw down the child's coffin from his shoulder. Then he said, "I may not win here. But I won't lose either."

Chapter 11 – A Chance to Fly

A Void tear. A hole in space, perhaps even time itself. Measuring but two yards in length, it hung in midair like a singular shelf without a wall. Visible only to the naked eye as a straight black line glowing with purplish supernatural energy, it would almost be easy to miss if not for it being high in the sky at the center of a hellscape most foul.

Said hellscape had developed initially around the tear's immediate influence and now well beyond it, aided by the musings of the Forbidden One. The Deep Woods, the surrounding swamps, and all the way to Parika' Te Mo had fallen to the sickening ways of this still-mysterious alien entity. The Void tear was at the center of all this; however, in its thousands of years of existence, it had never before tainted the lands beyond the Deep Woods as it was doing now.

Del'more Kar'dia is to blame, Quinn thought as he looked upon an artificial lake the size of a farmstead. With bare feet and no shirt upon his back, he bravely ventured to approach the alien organism that was consuming everything, alive and dead alike. Toward the monstrosity of the Void that planted itself at the lake's center, he marched. The last leg of his long journey to get revenge was finally here.

Quinn lifted his chin high to look up at the organism. His two blunt blades gripped tightly in each hand, he walked deeper into the lake until the alien bile, acidic in nature, was sloshing around his ankles, causing him a tingling pain.

Having left the coffin with the child at the shoreline, an exhausted but not yet defeated Quinn moved cautiously toward what he thought was the being he needed to slay. It was a towering hulk of gray-skinned flesh that, at first glance, looked like a flower, of all things. One which was over two hundred feet tall by Quinn's estimation. Disturbingly, it was made not of anything that looked like plant matter but of that wrinkly, hairy, alien flesh that smelled like a rotting carcass left out in the sun.

As sickly looking as all the forest around it, it was, no doubt, the source of the alien skin that somehow melted then consumed the Deep Woods at large. Quinn waded further through the ankle-deep lake of bile to the Deep Wood's center, trying not to throw up from the sickening smell. As he waded, he thought of how he would kill this fleshy plant monster, whose "petals" did not move by the wind but seemingly by their own chaotic volition. Perhaps it really was a type of animal, Quinn thought.

He came to the "flower's" base, and he expected to be attacked at any moment, but he was not. In fact, when he looked back at the shore not far yonder, he saw no Voidlings at all for the first time in hours. Was this not what they were all protecting? Quinn thought, greatly confused.

He looked back up at the flower of flesh and discerned that its petals were pointed squarely at the Void tear above it. Like a leaf that gains energy from the sun through photosynthesis, it must do a similar thing with the Void tear, Quinn thought. He looked down, dismayed, as he realized that this towering alien was way too big to kill with but two blunt—

"BLLLLLLLLAHHHHHHHHHKKKKKKKKKKK!!!!"

Roared a voice in Quinn's head as he turned from the "flower" in front of him to see a headless bird swooping down. Quinn almost panicked in that moment as the bird dropped low with its large wings spread wide. It glided with ease just above the shallow lake of black alien bile.

Quinn untensed a little as the headless rainbow-feathered bird came in to land but fifty yards from him. It landed with a splash of bile in a place between Quinn and the shoreline on which he left the coffined corpse, his only weapon against the creature who called itself Del'more Kar'dia.

The headless bird, the third and final Herald, then spread out its wings and stood as tall as a two-story inn. All one hundred of its creepy red, green, and purple eyes peered down at the comparatively small man before it. Quinn, realizing his mistake at the moment when it mattered most, said simply, "Fakk."

As if things couldn't get worse, a rushing breeze moved a silent purple fog out of the distant tree line and upon the murky alien-bile lake. The purple cloud rushed in and soon cut off all vision of the area. It was so thick that Quinn couldn't see the third Herald any longer, even though he knew it was still there.

He turned to his superhuman mutant sight, but that failed him also. As the moments passed and the fog grew thicker, he could no longer see past his hand in front of him.

"You wear the face of a king, yet you have no kingdom. You come before me bare-chested, covered in blood. Head to toe, you dress in the blood of your enemies. What am I to make of you, human? Are you a heartbroken Rogue Caster or the king of all barbarians alive?" said the voice of the young woman inside Quinn's head.

"I AM YOUR JUDGMENT!" Quinn roared with anger into the UVE fog before him, in the direction he last saw the third Herald.

"We'll see," she said as Quinn finally started to sense in his periphery the creatures that took Red. Quinn twisted around and brought both swords to bear as a blind, pig-headed short humanoid with four arms bearing three-fingered hands jumped at him from concealment in the whisking purple fog. Having the intention of pinning Quinn to the ground, it came at him with ferocity.

However, able to move quicker than his foul enemy, Quinn brought his two blunt blades together in a scissoring motion and offed its head with brute strength alone. As its small body fell with a splash of alien bile, Quinn heard something coming from behind. He twisted and blocked another of this fog's hunters from gripping him, quickly finding himself their new prey.

Quinn beat back the other one, able to move quicker than it because of his Gift power, but soon his advantage waned. As more and more of the blind creatures sensed his presence in their domain of rolling fog, they came at him. Once again, he was outnumbered.

"Is this yet another type of dreamed-up monster you have created here?!" Quinn said as he fought as they did, using sound and instinct alone against his many foes, now numbering at least eleven. Unfortunately for Quinn, without his sight he was fighting to maintain a stalemate, not secure a victory.

"No, these beings are real enough. Honestly, I didn't invite them here. Nobody ever invites the Phjukijak anywhere; they just sort of show up."

"My fight is with you, not them!" Quinn roared as a few of the Phjukijak jumped onto his back and started to scratch relentlessly at his exposed flesh, while others tried to grapple him to the ground yet still.

"Very well, I'll help," said the slightly condescending voice in Quinn's head.

As Quinn fought on, he felt the ground shake a little and heard a great splash of bile come from nearby. Quinn, with four pig-headed Phjukijak on his back, turned to see, in a flash of life before death, the still image of two open claws, those of a hawk almost taller than him.

He didn't even have time to curse as he was knocked off his feet, and the Phjukijak were, in turn, knocked off his back. Quinn was grabbed by the third Herald and spirited up just like Seppa had been a day ago. As he was lifted high above the UVE, the purple fog that the blind Phjukijak used to hunt with, he

145

realized that in the confusion of the moment, he had dropped not one but both swords.

"Don't mind their fog, it is no real threat. It is but smoke pretending to be wind. It's fake, like you are," said Del'more. Quinn as he was carried in the sharp claws very delicately, looked up at the hundreds of eyes on the third Herald's feathered underside.

Was this it? Was this monstrous bird really the Forbidden One? Quinn thought as he searched for the concealed leg strap that held his hidden dagger, his finishing blade, not stopping to care that a hundred alien eyes were watching him do so.

"Struggle against my claws all you like, mortal. You won't break free even with your Gift strength," Del'more said in Quinn's mind.

"What is your plan? To drop me just like my brother?"

"I might give you the chance to fly later, yes. But really, I brought you up here to talk. To show you something. I'd hate for you to think me unreasonable, and so I must put my proposition in terms even a human can understand."

"GIVE ME BACK MY BROTHERS!" Quinn roared, not wanting to hear a single word as the third Herald climbed higher and higher. At a point, it was high enough that you could see for fathoms upon fathoms in each direction. In that moment, high above the realm of mortal men, Quinn soberly realized that he could see further than any other man on the surface of the world.

He looked down and saw the new lake at the very center of the melting Deep Woods. He could see the large "flower" directly underneath the small Void tear. Beyond the lake and the flower, Quinn saw the swamps that he and his brothers had taken days to trek through. The very ones that neighbored Parika' Te Mo.

While Quinn could not see Parika' Te Mo directly because much of it lay under heavy tree cover, he could see in the far distance a man-made object beyond it. A single road. The Blue Road, the well-travelled main road leading to the capital city of Danneish. Bastone. He was amazed at how close it looked, in comparison to how long it would take for him to get there on foot.

"See, little human. Life has gone on in the world around you just as it did before. I have not taken much of your lands for myself. I have stopped my inhabitation at the borders of the town you used to call Parika' Te Mo."

"Inhabitation?"

"Yes. The Deep Woods shall become like my homeland. A single organism. I've looked at this world, this realm, for a hundred years, you see. Through the crack in the Void the ancient forbearers, the Peace Makers, left here. I like this reality well enough to want to put down permanent roots here. And as you can see below, I've even planted my first flower. Look at it, it's so pretty."

Quinn looked down at the melting forest and saw at its center the "flower" in question. He thought it couldn't conceivably be called pretty by anyone, nor anything for that matter. Was this the manner of curse to be brought further upon the Deep Woods? What other horrors would be planted here by the Forbidden One? Quinn thought in anguish.

"What is your purpose here, Del'more Kar'dia?" Quinn said sourly.

"Who are you, interloper, to question me on my purposes? You say I have come here to destroy, and I guess that I have. But know that my destruction has a higher purpose. For when a builder constructs a house for herself, she must first cut down a few trees. Tear a few stones from the ground, make level the foundations on which she will build her home.

"I am no destroyer of worlds, human. I am a being whose existence derives meaning from creation. Just like you claim you humans do, I exist to give meaning to a meaningless existence."

Quinn was silent for a moment. He still could not reach far back enough to get out his concealed blade. The wind rushing through his blood-covered hair, he was only half listening to what he interpreted as the Forbidden One's plea to him for existence. A plea Quinn had no real desire to indulge.

"I don't believe you to be a being of peace! Your actions speak louder than your words!" Quinn roared with rage.

"Do you think me a fictional monster? A fairy tale villain?" the young woman's voice said with great offense. "Your human skulls will serve as coal in my heart's furnace. I burn with majesty as lesser races die at my hand," she said in a throaty impression of what she thought a "real" monstrous villain should sound like. "Is that the sort of language you expect from one such as I?" she then said normally.

"I expect you to die!" Quinn struggled against the sharp claws of the headless hawk, cutting himself in the process.

"Look at you, king of barbarians, of humanity. Lost in your feelings to the extent that you neither see nor comprehend simple logic anymore. Unlike you, I am not bound by the paradigm of human emotion or your array of limited senses through which you perceive our shared reality. I am beyond such things as you, man of humanity's judgment. Why must you make me suffer through your delusions of grandeur? See sense!"

"You claim to perceive so much, yet you do not see the obvious in front of you."

"That being?" Del'more said angrily.

"That because we are so alien to you, you are thus alien to us. You claim to understand us, yet you make no attempt to in any real way. You must have observed us, yes. The goings-on of the people of Parika' Te Mo? Yet did you try to speak with any of the villagers before you slew them? Did the thought even occur to you in your hundred years of watching us? I wager not."

The Forbidden One was silent for a moment, prompting Quinn to continue.

"You infer yourself wiser than any human. But if you were, you wouldn't have acted as an observer from the sidelines for over a hundred years. You would have expanded your knowledge of this new world you've come to claim partial ownership of by mutually beneficial interaction, not by judging from afar and then making dangerous assumptions."

"I think you've just started talking about yourself, human."

"YES! I admit it! If what you say about your true purpose in this world is true, then we have made the same kind of dangerous assumptions about you. Which, again, proves my point," Quinn said in anger. Del'more was silent for a contemplative moment.

"Finally, human . . . I understand you. You say that if I had approached humanity in peace a hundred years ago, this all wouldn't have had to happen. Maybe . . . Maybe not. I do not know," Del'more said, sounding like she was still deep in thought.

As Quinn stopped struggling due to the massive cuts it was causing along his body, his battle rage, not being able to vent, started to subside. As his rage lowered, so did his torrent of hateful emotions. They peeled back to reveal logic and reason.

"Would you believe it, human, if I said that all I have done has been because of my ignorance of humanity?" the young woman's voice in Quinn's head said softly. Quinn sighed.

"Human law does not work on the basis of ignorance. It applies to all, even those who do not understand it. What you have done, oh woman of the Void, has been in ignorance of the laws of man. Both written and unwritten. That is why you are worthy of being slain. That is one of the reasons why I detest you."

"Why should I, one who is not human, bow down to the laws of mankind? Why should a superior being in both years and mental capability like myself, subjugate herself to your solely human rules and considerations?" Del'more said not with anger but truly as if she was trying to understand the truth of it.

"For the sake of survival, for the sake of coexistence, you must follow the rules of the household you live in," said Quinn, his exhaustion from the day's great battles catching up to him.

"You demand something of me to coexist with you? Am I not allowed to do the same?"

"And what did you demand from humanity then? Nothing. My brothers' lives, the villagers of Parika' Te Mo, the Deep Woods and its surroundings. You just took all you wanted without any words."

Quinn looked down with sadness upon the Deep Woods and the surrounding corrupted area, at everything Del'more thought she was naturally entitled to. The being may have been wise and supremely intelligent, but she was an ignoramus in the ways of the human mind and world.

"Fine, I admit wrongdoing on my part. Now that I've conceded a measure of guilt, let me go. Let me have the peaceful coexistence with you humans that you alluded to the possibility of just before. All I really want is the land here, nothing else."

"I said that if you truly were a being of creation like we humans are, then there could be peace. But I know, simply from the fact that you came from the Void itself, that you are not that. Ten times over. There cannot be peace with you, ever! Between what you are and what humanity is, oh being of death. Former denizen of a graveyard. You are Void! You are our antithesis!"

At Quinn's harsh words, Del'more removed all friendliness, all girlishness from her telepathic young woman's voice. She made one demand of Quinn, and she made it plainly.

"Burn that body of the little girl. Then burn the idea from your mind that you can put me into it. Then, and only then, will I consider not torturing you for the rest of time and existence itself, you immortal man."

"Do it. I can endure pain longer than you can keep torturing me. Only one of us is truly immortal, remember."

At Quinn's defiant words, Del'more screamed with anger into his mind. Then the third and final Herald, who was the long-awaited Forbidden One herself, dropped Quinn from a few fathoms above the earth. Keeping her word and giving Quinn a "chance to fly." Like the rest of Quinn's trouble-ridden life, it was a chance he never wanted but got anyway.

***

Quinn landed with a splash and a crack of bone. The purple fog had receded as its Phjukijak masters found no prey within it and so moved on. Quinn was once again alone in the middle of the bile lake in the heat of the boiling sun. Except this time, he was crushed into a heap of bone and flesh by his violent fall. Having broken his back, his legs, and even his arms, he looked up in immeasurable pain to the cloudless, sweaty sky above.

Worse off in that moment than a paraplegic, as his neck was broken as well, he saw in his periphery the headless rainbow hawk as it flew overhead.

"You fly terribly, human," Del'more said mockingly. With growing anger, Quinn gathered his Caster energy, his inner warmth. As he did so, Del'more positioned herself nearby with a graceful landing.

As she touched down, Quinn released his inner warmth, and with great pain and exhaustion, he tried to stand up slowly. His back snapped back into place, and the broken bones in his legs pushed themselves back into his body. This allowed him to finally stand with a great, anguished effort.

His arms cracked back into place, and the flesh surrounding his bones seemingly boiled itself back into existence as it healed. A blood-soaked and now bile-soaked Quinn remade himself before Del'more, who towered above him a hundred yards away on her large bird-clawed legs.

"Do you know the difference between a hunter and a trapper?" said Del'more, still using telepathy to talk.

Quinn snapped his broken neck back into place as he turned to face the thing he hated.

"A hunter pursues their foe. A trapper waits and lets it come to them," he said, unimpressed, as he reached into his leg strap for his only weapon, a seven-inch dagger commonly and aptly called a finishing blade.

"Huh, it's true then. I am like that Rogue Caster you killed when your Akuan first came to what was called Parika' Te Mo. I am a trapper, you a hunter. Our approaches are different, yet the effect is the same: dead prey."

"I am nothing like you," Quinn all but growled in defiance as he looked past the towering Voidling bird to the coffin of Debbie's child, which was still on the shore, seemingly untouched.

"I have you trapped just where I want you, in a lake of goo without any cover in sight," said Del'more as she spread her wings, revealing the hundreds of creepy eyes on her feathered underside.

"It's as you said. I'm a hunter, not a trapper. I need no homefield advantage to slay," a deadly serious Quinn said as he entered an at-the-ready fighting stance. He held a closed fist where a buckler would normally be. Then with great conviction and the flexing of bloodied superhuman muscles, he let himself smile a little. He then opened his fist into a come-at-me gesture.

His overt confidence prompted Del'more to scream in his mind, trying to pop his head off with thoughts. The great headless bird she was slunk down. Then with a roar of air and a mighty heave of bird leg, she took off from the ground and came at him. The telepathic scream, which made Quinn's ears bleed until he was deaf, was no concern to Quinn. He gritted through the pain of his mind melting from a noise he couldn't escape, then dashed forward. He charged her as she charged him.

The two, having finally said all they needed to say, having finally understood each other totally yet having chosen not to care, chose to rush the being opposite. Like a collision of realities that could not mix, only one of them could win this battle between a champion of life and a champion of death. Only one. Or so it appeared.

The razor-sharp claws came at Quinn just like he knew they would. Just like he saw with Seppa and then again with himself when he was kidnapped to the sky. Being predictable was Del'more's great mistake. For while her claws could slash and kill any mortal man, Quinn, humanity's champion, was not mortal in the least.

So when the headless bird came at Quinn, who ran through the bile lake toward her incoming claws, Quinn charged onward with a smile upon his blood-soaked face. For he, the hunter of men, of beast, of Voidling, and now even death incarnate, was now all but certain he could win.

The claws came in, and Quinn jumped with glee into them. He was sliced in half, his intestines falling from his belly, yet he had accomplished his aim. As the bird pulled up into the sky just like it had before, something was different. Del'more looked down at her underside in great surprise as she saw a bloodied barbarian hanging, clinging to her rainbow-colored feathers.

Before she could even react, Quinn took the finishing blade from his teeth and stabbed hard into Del'more's underside, causing her to let out another bloodcurdling, telepathic screech, one that Quinn could no longer hear in his mind. For the part of his brain that could thus be adversely affected had been destroyed by all the nonstop telepathic screaming from Del'more.

To combat this, Quinn simply stopped regenerating the speech cognition center of his brain. In doing so, he stopped her abuse of telepathy, and his mind was his own once again.

Quinn saw a satisfying amount of a black, blood-like substance leak out of the large gash he made on Del'more's feathered underside. She pulled hard to the right to try and flick the half of a man that was Quinn off.

She rolled in the air, but Quinn used what little inner warmth he had left to power his Gift strength. Acting like a tick on her belly, he wouldn't let go as he stung.

Quinn bit again into her underside with his finishing blade as he held on for dear life, this time cutting through a line of eyeballs. Bells, they gushed with black blood, Quinn thought as he smiled wickedly; the villain in this moment truly was him.

Del'more, losing more and more blood by the moment, got desperate enough to dive toward the ground, understanding that it was now or never to recover from this one-sided brawl. She didn't understand before, but to her horror, she did now; because Quinn was immortal, he could lose a fight and yet still win.

She dived, losing yards upon yards of altitude in mere moments. Quinn, with the voracity of a madman, held on and, worse for her still, stabbed and stabbed and stabbed some more! The black blood gushed out of her as she roared into a brain that could no longer fathom words, perhaps not even conscious thoughts. Only killer instinct.

Del'more, the Forbidden One, the sentient Voidling who killed the stern Second Adjunct Fredstar. The surgeon Michael. The aloof but well-meaning giant called Bryon. His jokester brother Tryan. The thief called Red. The deadeye called Seppa. The charming First Adjunct Samson. The mentor and father to the Silver Serpents, Tar. And finally, the loudmouth Gus and the humble, God-fearing Orranian called Lichale, who pronounced his *S*'s as *Z*'s.

The one who had slayed them all not only by her own hand or claw but also by her devious planning knew in that moment as she fell, not flew, down from the sky. She knew she was undone. She realized she had had failed.

Quinn rode the now crippled rainbow-colored bird to the bile below with a splash and mighty crash. She came in along the ground and ran ashore, throwing all manner of filth into the air. Her final resting place, chosen perhaps by fate, was just before the coffin of Debbie's child that Quinn had left ashore.

Having survived the second fall from the sky by sheer determination, the half of Quinn that was still leaking intestines behind him crawled. Yes, crawled up on the top of the headless bird and started to cut down the center of her back. Both hands on the finishing blade, Quinn gritted his teeth as he went searching not for a lost soul, but a lost hope.

"Pleasssse . . . Pleasee! Come bac fro da deada liks ou id in Pel's airy ale . . . Youuuu can'ttt die this easy! I'm not done with you yet!" Quinn said aloud as his brain's cognition center regenerated itself. Quinn found nothing inside the alien monster except more black blood. Not flesh, not even a spine or a single bone could he find within it.

He thought he'd at least find a nexus of nerves within her body to help him pinpoint the location of this sentient's brain, which she must still have. But alas, it was no use. The entity was hollow but for the black blood. This alien creature had biology unlike anything humanity had seen before.

Failing to confirm the killing blow to this now motionless, headless corpse, Quinn looked over his shoulder. Not far from him, he could see the lower half of his body floating in the ankle-deep lake of black, alien bile.

Quinn, using his numbed arms and hands, pushed off the large corpse of the bird and leapt into the bile lake with a mucky splash. Feeling weaker and weaker as his battle fury wore off, Quinn slithered like a snake, like a serpent.

As he moved toward his slowly dissolving lower half, he struggled and struggled, fighting exhaustion and pain all the way. In the end, he got to his lower half just in time. And with the last of his inner warmth, he made himself whole. Five tired minutes later, he crawled up on the shore beside the Forbidden One's corpse. Beside the coffin of Debbie's daughter.

It was then and only then that Quinn's strength, his anger, waned. It was then that Quinn stepped down as champion of humanity, of life itself, and became something more humble and ordinary. In that prideful moment upon the shore of a bile lake, having, to his eye, finally defeated the cause of all his vexation, Quinn let himself become human again. He let his extreme exhaustion take him. The living blade that he was sheathed itself into blissful unconsciousness; he slept.

Chapter 12 – Those That Never Return

Quinn awoke upon a sandy shore. The stars were out in infinite number, shining like beacons of light within a black, all-encompassing Void. To Quinn, each star held a poetic meaning. Each was a lighthouse of brilliance to navigate by in a dark, dreary world. He sincerely wished and above all hoped to be such a beacon.

Am I dreaming? was Quinn's first thought. With great pain, he lifted his head from the ground. He was badly sunburned, and his skin cracked with a lack of moisture. In the distance, past the black bile lake, he saw the hairy alien "flower" still there, directly under the tear, wriggling in its disconcerting way.

No, I am not dreaming, Quinn thought unhappily. He mustered his energy and sat up, then realized he was not alone. He saw a child, a young girl with long brown hair and ragged clothes. She smelled like death itself. Quinn's mind, still fumbling from sleepiness, didn't immediately understand who or what she was. Only when he looked around and saw the child's coffin that lay beside him now empty, did he understand what had happened.

He rubbed his eyes in shock as he confirmed what he saw in front of him, the girl playing hopscotch upon the sandy shore. Where there was once only death, he now saw hope incarnate.

"I . . . knew . . ." Quinn struggled to speak because of his dry mouth.

"Drink up human, so you can speak. Finally, let us make our accord," said an all-too-familiar voice in Quinn's head as he miraculously found a full waterskin in his hand that seemingly appeared from nowhere.

Quinn, hardheaded and one to look a gift horse squarely in the mouth, threw down the waterskin onto the sand in defiance as he stood from the ground. He licked his lips, trying to force salivation in his dry mouth.

"Stay where you are. Let me end this, Del'more. Let me slay you for the final time. Just as we imagined we needed to at the start of all this bullshit."

The little girl, Debbie's dead daughter, reanimated by the possession of an alien, stopped her hopscotch and looked at Quinn with haunting eyes. Eyes which surprisingly seemed very human. Despite having been dead for over a week, Debbie's daughter still looked undeniably human. It irked Quinn and discomforted him to no end.

Not because of how disgusting a reanimated corpse was to see in the flesh, but because it proved that even the Forbidden One, a being that represented death incarnate to Quinn, could still appear somewhat human. Could come in a form similar to his. Quinn walked closer to the brown-haired child, who had withered flowers still left in her hair from her burial.

"Us humans and you Void folk are like oil and water. We do not mix. If you shall not leave, you must die. Your happiness is not worth the happiness of all humanity."

"That's exactly what they are going to say when they finally come for you, Rogue Caster," Debbie's daughter said, to Quinn's great surprise, in her little girl's voice. It seemed that when Del'more had access to a mouth, she could indeed use it. And use it pointedly at that.

Quinn hesitated for a moment as the dusty-haired girl showed great fear when he approached her. Before he got to her, his hands each a tight fist, Debbie's daughter tripped in the sand as she retreated and fell on her back in front of him. It was now Quinn's turn to tower over her.

"Can we talk about this, mister? Pretty please? We can find common ground, I'm sure," said the poor, defenseless-looking girl. Quinn had to keep reminding himself that she was very much not that at all.

"One cannot find common ground with death."

"And what if I'm not death? What if I am just another kind of lifeform in this universe? What if you are wrong?" the little girl said as Quinn stood firm.

"I think the greater question here is, what if I am right? What if you are everything you say you aren't? Why would a being of your power stop at the end of the Deep Woods? At the end of Parika' Te Mo. In a universe as large and empty as ours, you want only a tiny piece of land to yourself? To find a quiet peace that happens to be right here with us humans? I don't believe you; it's absurd. The human world is anything but peaceful."

"It's the truth! I just want to watch from a distance! I want to watch this world—"

"Burn," Quinn said, interrupting her, having finally zeroed in on the Forbidden One's true intention. Del'more tried to hide it, but Quinn saw the tiny smirk she made when he mentioned that word.

"Yourself is the only thing you will own from the beginning to the end of your life. I hope you've used it well." Quinn leaned down and grabbed Del'more's weak new form by her ragged clothes.

"Stop! I'll give you what you really want!" Del'more screamed in panic as she recoiled unsuccessfully from Quinn, about to go in for a finishing punch. A punch that would see Del'more ended—forever—this time round.

"Don't give me that! You said you couldn't give me what I truly wanted!" Quinn raged, his tight, bloodied fist looming in the air above the possessed child.

"I lied!" Del'more screamed back.

"You'll say anything, absolutely anything to escape your just punishment. Prove it to me!" Quinn roared back, the tension between them having reached its crescendo.

"I can't! You'll kill me afterward! Once I give you what you want, you'll kill me!"

"You should be so lucky to enjoy a quick death. Maybe I should subject you to the same mental torture and despair you made me and my brothers live through!"

Del'more wept loudly like the little girl she wasn't, truly afraid to die at Quinn's hand. Whatever spell, whatever Void curse she had placed on the Deep Woods affected her the same as everything else. Quinn imagined Del'more would finally die when he punched her in her face, crushing her skull. Thus, reality would change to match what the only human left standing from the Deep Woods to Parika' Te Mo, adamantly believed.

"Who are you really?" Quinn said, shaking the corpse violently. "Is Del'more Kar'dia even your real name?! It sounds too human to truly be yours. Did you lie about that too? Did you try and steal somebody's identity as well?"

The jig was up. Quinn, the Nameless Man, had seen through all her veils and found the Forbidden One to be, at her heart, a liar and thief as well as a murderer of men she didn't understand, nor cared to.

Quinn, overcome by emotion, having not enough moisture to shed more tears for his dead friends, shed tears of blood instead, which rolled down his cheeks and onto the small girl. Through his great pain, Quinn said simply, "I am your judgment. I have come to collect."

At Quinn's parting words, Del'more finally relented. She snapped her fingers, and in a moment, the scene around them drastically changed. No longer did they sit upon the shore of a bile lake. No longer was there a towering hairy "flower" from another world sunbathing before a Void tear. No longer was the ancient forest all around them melting into an alien-skinned ground.

Quinn was shocked. Everything was as he remembered before. The Deep Woods, as he knew it when he first ventured here seemingly so long ago, had now returned fully. Not a tree, not a leaf, not even a blade of grass was missing from his memory of it. Nor did it look like it had ever been disturbed. The Forbidden One had done it. She had brought back the habitat of humanity, the clothes of our human world.

"See . . . I can do more, you know," Del'more said with a quiet, fleeting voice. Quinn was visibly shaken by this sudden reversal of fiction into fact. Del'more had brought back life from death, purely out of his memories. His hope against all hope for his brothers' return, his desire that he feared impossible as Del'more had previously said, now changed from illogical hope to definite possibility. Could what had been taken from him truly be returned?

"Who or what are you to have power over life and death?" Quinn said, his voice trembling as he continued to believe desperately that there was a way to get his brothers back from death. Back from her.

"I have no power over life or death. Only over belief itself. I have only the powers your human mind gives me in this realm."

"I don't believe you!" Quinn's logical self cried out as he struggled within himself.

"The creation of a belief is always more interesting than the belief itself. Your logical mind believes me not, but the other part of you, your heart, believes. Where do you think, human, your interpretation of existence comes from? Your head or your heart? I don't know about the rest of your kind, but as for you, you are all heart."

"Impossible, I am not that man."

"Your heart betrays you. It wants you to give in to me. It wants to negotiate your brothers' return," Del'more said quietly for fear of inciting rage within the man of judgment called Quinn.

In that moment, Quinn's logical self and his sorrowful heart fought a battle for control of his mind and his interpretation of reality. He desperately wanted to give in to her demand for

161

mercy, one which would come at the gain of his brothers' lives and perhaps even those of the slayed residents of Parika' Te Mo.

However, his logical self argued that it was plain wrong for this liar, this thief, this murderer and torturer of men to live but a single second more. Quinn had a law to uphold, one higher than the laws of men, that of vengeance itself. Surely, he could not part with his new reason for being to bring back his old purpose in life? Surely . . .

"Come on, you know you want your brothers back. As healthy and mentally fit as the day they departed from this realm, I could give them to you. Who cares about justice, really? You probably think me a liar; that I am, yes. You infer me a thief; that I am, yes. You call me a murderer, a torturer of men; that I am, yes. But let me tell you that you have done just as much wrong as I, if not more. You simply do not remember."

"Liar, I lived as a good man in my past life," Quinn said quietly, his rage finally failing him.

"Believe what you want, human; only in this forest will it become true. In the time I've been watching you humans, I realized that not one of you, not one, is strong enough to abide by your own contrived philosophy."

"I am not a real human. I'm a Rogue Caster; I'm a mutant."

"You think like a human; therefore, you are a human. Despite what your corrupted biology might tell you," Del'more said, more strong-willed than before, sensing that she was getting under Quinn's skin with her arguments.

"It would be wrong to let you live . . ." Quinn mumbled as his fist lowered to the ground and he released his grasp on Del'more's ragged clothes.

"It's like you said to Telligood. There is always justifiable reason, isn't there? To do what is wrong."

"It still doesn't make it right."

"It still doesn't make it the wrong choice. The law of men, I don't understand it well. But I do understand it's not perfect.

162

Why judge someone to death when you can forgive them? Give them an opportunity to change instead. Is that not what a being whose life's purpose is creation, not destruction, would do? Come on, human, prove you are a better being than I am."

At Del'more's smooth, silky words, Quinn got more caught up in the moment, and he relaxed back on the grassy ground. His eyes a million fathoms away, lost in thought. The pitch-darkness of the forest filled the quiet moment for a while until Quinn broke it with these simple words.

"Give me back everything. Then you shall live."

Del'more sat up and looked Quinn squarely in the eye. Her confidence in herself returning moment by moment, she smiled.

"You'll let me go? Truly? And what of the other men I've killed? The villagers. The Foresters, the search party sent after them. That little girl, whom I lured into that well. Whose body I wear now. What about their justice? What about the justice for the dead you drove yourself into a frenzy over? How can I be sure you won't just kill me once I bring back some of the dead?"

"You can't bring them all back? I thought you'd be able to bring back everyone you killed, not just my brothers."

"This would be a compromise. I can't give you everything you want. My pride stops me from admitting utter defeat just as your pride does the same for you."

"You'd keep them dead for your pride's sake? You are truly despicable. What that means is that you will have human blood on your hands. Humans cannot forgive that easily. They'll still see you as their enemy for as long as you reside here."

"Such a thing is natural, is it not? I am of the Void," Del'more said cheekily. "I'll give you back your brothers and the lives of everyone who died by my hand at Parika' Te Mo. That is, except this little girl, whose form I shall now wear. Not one more."

"Then I shall impose my own prideful condition. You must now do as your lies inscribed before. You are forever limited to stay within the realm of the Deep Woods, which will exist as it is now. You shall lift your imagined curse on these lands forever. Break these terms, and I will come back. I will hunt you and kill you yet again. For good."

"Agreed. Yet you still have not answered my question. How will you exact your justice from me once I bring back the dead?" Del'more asked as she watched Quinn stand. So she did as well.

"The dead get no justice. It's something only the living can acquire. Good men being able to live once more is a greater justice to me than killing a pathetic creature like you. If I must pay for justice with the currency of forgiving great evils, then I shall pay it. With great effort and great reluctance, I shall pay that high price. Dearly," Quinn said with a sour look on his face, disgusted at this choice he was making.

Del'more smiled with glee, satisfied with his answer. The alien in the little girl's form walked up to Quinn with her hand out to shake. To seal the agreement as humans naturally do. Quinn, despite himself, despite almost every fiber in his body telling him it was wrong, extended his hand for the shake. But, good sense returning to him, he retracted it at the last moment as his conflicting desires waged war within.

Is this really me? To give into evil, to be bribed by death in return for the thing it itself took from me? Wouldn't the Forbidden One be the only one to profit from this trade? It does not care in the slightest for my brothers' lives, only for its own self-preservation and its right to watch our world burn. It gets everything it wants in this deal; I get back only what little it stole from me.

Bells! What did Tar say in that suspect vision to me just after his death? That there will be a choice at the end of this story. One I will not wish to make.

The words of Tar came back to Quinn as he realized that choice was now: "I ask that when you choose between the two bad options presented, you will choose the one that will cause you the most pain. Choose pain over what feels good in the

164

moment, my friend, for that is the path of righteousness," Tar's old wise-sounding voice said in his head.

But, Tar! I want to do what is right yet can't! I don't want to kill! I never truly have. Quinn fell to his knees, his face to the ground before the Forbidden One, who looked down at the man she broke with but words.

I want to be something other than a blade, Tar. I never wanted to become the judgment of the dead. I never chose to become a killing machine; I was simply born into this world as one. Surely, Tar, voice from the grave. Surely not yet another death is the way forward. Surely forgiveness must also have its day.

Quinn looked up to Del'more, the withered funeral flowers still falling out of her brown hair. He raised his hand to hers from a kneel, matching her eye level. He said to himself, finally justifying all that he wanted to believe: *surely it is better to forgive than it is to condemn.*

Quinn shook Del'more's small hand. The accord of the Deep Woods that holds even now was struck. Humanity and the being from the Void had brokered a peace once thought to be impossible. All it cost was the judgment of humanity, which many may say was too high a price. But alas, you and I were not there that day. You and I did not conquer death incarnate, nor lose their entire beloved Akuan to it just earlier that day.

You and I can judge Quinn all we like, but only he was worthy of making the choice. Wrong or otherwise. Even I, his former Akuan brother and greatest of friends, believe that our man Quinn made the wrong choice here. That he made a totally selfish decision. One that went against the wills of his fallen brothers even.

However, I know that our Quinn, the Nameless Man, who didn't even know at this point who or what he truly was, I know that when deciding between the fate of the world and the fate of his friends, he chose the latter. He chose to give in to his feelings and depart from the path of righteousness he so labored to stay

165

upon. All that being said, I don't think anyone anywhere blames him for this act. I certainly do not.

The game was rigged from the start; both choices led to a loss. Del'more made sure of that. She could not win in combat, so she defeated him on the moral high ground. Quinn stood up again, having finally committed himself fully to the act of forgiveness.

Despite his logical self, he said to her, "I choose to give you grace in this moment. One which you do not deserve nor have earned." Quinn then started to force himself to believe in his empty words. "For you have convinced me now that you are not some being destined to do evil deeds. Just a creature of terrible habits inclined to make wicked mistakes. I've changed my mind about you."

Yes, Quinn thought. He could not kill her, but perhaps he could change her by the power that made her mortal. The power of belief itself. He continued, picking up with enthusiasm in his tone.

"You were right before. With your arguments, you've convinced me we are indeed alike. You may not be human, but you make the same mistakes we all do. I believe there is hope for you yet."

Del'more smiled. Perhaps she understood Quinn's counterattack against her, perhaps she didn't. All she knew for sure was that Quinn had finally let his feelings guide his logic. He had truly listened to her, and now she finally felt safe in our realm.

Quinn continued, "What you do with your life that I have given you, within the conditions agreed upon, is up to you. But let me say this. For you, peace is always an option. At least for someone like you, who still has the capacity to choose to be something other than a living weapon, something other than a blade in human form like I am."

"I know it means almost nothing to you, human. But I came to watch your world burn, not to help burn it. At my heart, and yes, we Voidlings have one or two, I am a scientist above all else, an observer of truths. I am as you are, not perfect. Let us broken beings harm each other no more."

"Go, do no harm. As I will do no more to you."

Del'more smiled genuinely, and Quinn's heart sank once more. He had both lost and won at the same time. Just as she had. He didn't know how he felt about that. Bells, his counterattack might not even work. In that moment, he remembered the Fifth Silver Serpent Oath.

It said to be kind to the stranger, the wayfarer, the unknown quantity along the journey. For good is rewarded with good, and absence of mercy is rewarded in turn. Hopefully, his act of uncharacteristic kindness would add more good to this world. He shook his head at the thought as he looked down at his bloodied bare feet. Probably not.

What would he tell his brothers when they asked him what happened to the Forbidden One? They did what he could not. They sacrificed themselves all for the greater good of humanity. To beat back the Void but another day. He, however, was not strong enough. What did Lichale once say? Obedience against one's own will is the ultimate sacrifice. Bells, he failed that twice. Once to his Akuan, the second time to himself.

Quinn looked up suddenly from his heavy thoughts. Where was she? Del'more had completely disappeared in the night!

About to swear out a curse, Quinn felt something on his hands and realized he was wearing gloves. Not any gloves but the personally fitted ones he had lost five days ago in a swampy bog. From his hands, he saw sleeves of a shirt; then, as he looked down at himself in the dark, he saw not his bloody chest but his padded Silver Serpent under armor connected to his dark green forest cloak. All the items that he had thought were lost forever had been put back on him without action or word. Even his boots were back, polished cleaner than ever.

Quinn rested his hand on his belt and found his blade in its sheath. He drew it and with amazement found it was as sharp as the day it was forged. Suddenly, out of nowhere, a great light came toward him from between the trees. The ball of light came in and reformed itself into a rainbow of bright, vibrant colors. Del'more then reinvented herself in a kaleidoscope of color, illuminating the dark forest like never before.

With a dropped jaw, Quinn saw a young woman emerge from the almost blinding light. Dressed in spiraling colors, she all but danced in the air with her magnificence, her beauty; it was like nothing Quinn had ever seen before.

"Put away that blade. Don't go backing out of our accord now," Del'more, now the being of bright lights, said to Quinn, using the mouth on her new human form.

"Is this what you really look like?" Quinn said with a quiet suspicion.

"I can look like anything your human mind can imagine. It's rather telling that this is your imagined hope of what I would one day become."

"A being of only light. A beacon in utter darkness . . . I guess that's what I also want for myself," said Quinn humbly.

Del'more smiled and then extended her hand to Quinn as she leaned toward him in the air. Her brown hair in a girlish braid with living flowers tied within, the young woman was almost certainly the grown-up version of Debbie's dead child. She smiled at him as if they were old friends.

Del'more's smile still seemed alien to Quinn. Almost as if there was nothing underneath it. No bones, no muscles. No blood nor flesh of any kind, just as with her headless bird form. Only this time, she was filled not with black blood but bright light.

Despite being clothed in shining lights, her skin and body was human-looking in its complexion. While she was completely still, she looked normal despite her otherworldly clothes. Her long dress. She was indistinguishable from a real human at a distance.

However, as she moved toward him slowly, her human face became like a tablecloth over an invisible table. The covering made it seem like it was there, but if you looked under it, you'd see nothing at all. At least, that was the impression she gave Quinn. He really didn't wish to cut into her to see what was inside this time round. That is, unless he really needed to. So instead of more violence, he sheathed his sword and with great reluctance took Del'more's extended hand.

"Thanks for imagining me so pretty. This beats the first form you humans gave me by much," Del'more said cheekily.

"What now?" Quinn said, not wanting to engage any more with this creature than he had to.

Del'more smiled another of her favorite cheeky smiles, obviously enjoying her new face. She released her grasp from Quinn's hand and moved both of her palms to the cheeks upon his face. She said these words as she shut her eyes, prompting Quinn to do the same.

"Believe for me, Quinn. Believe that this was all just a bad dream. An unreality made up of fear, not substance. Believe in the hope that you alone held dear, that almost all that was lost can perhaps be found again."

In that moment, Quinn set all his being onto the thought of hope. He cast his broken heart down. Then earnestly believed that every word the Forbidden One said was indeed true. It was just a bad dream. One which he could then wake up from. Then, by the mysteriousness of the Void, all that was said and done was undone.

Or perhaps you could say it was never done in the first place. All the memories that both Quinn and Del'more shared of this bad ending for all became a premonition of a future and past that would never come into this reality, into this timeline or world.

Quinn's dream became reality; the former reality became but a dream. That was Del'more's great power; that was the Forbidden One's curse. And so Quinn opened his eyes, finding himself not standing but lying upon the weed-ridden forest floor. He woke from the dream and into the new reality, the new world. In the light of Del'more's shining clothes, he was the first one awake of many—of eleven sleeping men wearing dark green forest cloaks.

"Arh fakk . . ." he heard Gus say as he too awoke from the forest floor.

"I feel like death," said Samson as he stirred awake.

"I feel hungry," said Bryon, his stomach speaking with a growl before his mouth had chance to.

"What's that blinding light?" asked Fredstar as he bought up his hand to shield his eyes from Del'more's vibrantly colored clothes.

"Quinn? Is that you?" said a sleepy Tryan as he watched the oddest event in the world's history appear before him. The always serious man, whether from a momentary lapse in judgment or a bout of madness, did something he had never done before. Not even the strange sight of an unknown angelic woman dressed in beautiful lights could distract his brothers from the display Quinn was putting on in front of them all. For this angel descending from the heavens above seemed normal in comparison, more ordinary than Quinn in this moment.

Quinn saw that all ten of his brothers were back from the dead, alive in the flesh, cursing and complaining as they always did, all slightly confused, having been taken from when they died, into the now. Quinn did the opposite of what you might expect of our sorrowful hero to do. He did something that was totally uncharacteristic of him.

Overcome with glee, overcome with the realization that he was no longer all alone, he got up and danced with joy. He danced with joy before all ten of his bewildered brothers, before even the Forbidden One, his nemesis whom he forgave despite himself.

He danced to no tune other than the natural rhythm of life itself. He ripped off his cloak, his under armor and shirt; he leapt for joy in front of his brothers, who understood nothing at that point, especially how they all got there. Still confused and questioning, they all stopped to watch with smiles and laughter while their celebrating, probationary brother Quinn danced with pure, madness-induced joy.

You see, at the moment they saw him dancing with a great smile upon his face, they knew everything was going to be okay. Everything was as it was, and that was just okay with them. In that moment, they no longer cared what had happened, for they understood that them all being together like this was to be richly celebrated. And so, feeling the joy inherent to all life, Tar was the first to join the madman called Quinn in his uproar of bad dancing.

Samson soon joined in on the madness too. Then Bryon and Tryan, not giving a "fakk." Gus then Red, who cannot dance at all. They too joined the weed-ridden dancefloor of dirt. Bells, even Seppa got off his high horse as he laughed and joined them in making merry. Locking arms with some of his brothers as they swung round and round and round. Laughing at the stupidness of it all.

Even Fredstar, a picture of seriousness, found it in himself in the moment to do a little jig. The Forbidden One, the young hollow woman from another world, laughed at the humans dancing to no song and then decided to provide one to accompany their movements.

Yes, you heard me. They danced and sang in the presence of their enemy, and they were all delighted. Quinn did what none of us ever thought possible in that moment, he stopped fighting death for a moment and made peace with the Void. I can't help but hope that in that moment of craziness, of unbridled joy, that the alien, the liar, the thief, the murderer of men, saw in humanity something other than pain, suffering, and greed.

Just as I hope you, dear reader, see in this moment (which convinced me of the need to write this book) that the Nameless Man, my lost Akuan brother, my greatest friend, is not the monster other historians would have you believe. The being of sole evil everyone everywhere makes him out to be is but fiction meant to enrich the prideful and cover the real truth.

The Nameless Man, the alleged greatest villain in our world's entire history, danced with joy in the presence of his enemy, who he learned to forgive. For the sake of a selfish plea to never be alone, to bring back those he loved, his brothers, his only friends. This campaign started with a death. It ended with a dance and a song of utter joy.

Chapter 13 – Dead Men Tell No Tales

"Remember, laddies, not a single word," said Commander Tar with great seriousness in a low voice as he and all ten of his Silver Serpent Akuan brothers entered the sleepy village of Parika' Te Mo, a town which was eerily just as they had all first found it thirteen days ago.

Children played in puddles by the only road through town. The Pothole pub looked like it could collapse in on itself at any moment, like usual. A team of craftsmen and their young sons worked on constructing a new boat out of recently cut planks in front of their small shack of a strong house. Swamp fish were drying in the sun where the light was not blocked by the tall mangroves above. Fishermen's wives swore at their husbands for being lazy, commanding them to go back to work.

Bells! Quinn thought, *it's like what happened in the Deep Woods. Everything destroyed by Del'more has returned to a state of predestruction. The state that, before my lived experience turned premonition, existed only in my memories of the past.*

After a few more steps from all the bewildered brothers, almost all of whom distinctly remembered seeing this village horribly destroyed, Tar was flagged down by the village head and some elders of Parika' Te Mo. They all inquired as to the status of the threat at the heart of the Deep Woods.

Tar said simply, "It has been satiated."

As Tar, Second Adjunct Fredstar, and First Adjunct Samson gathered with the elder villagers to explain just what that meant, the rest of the Silver Serpents gathered in their own little huddle, away from prying ears.

"This is creepy. It's like they don't even remember dying," said Tryan, a dispirited look on his face.

"No, this isn't creepy, it's fakked. They get to forget dying, but I don't? Bloody unfair that is," said Gus, complaining to all his brothers present.

"Think of the children here. It's best they don't remember what the pain of death feels like," said Lichale, the most compassionate of their number.

"Aye. I still have nightmares about that headless bird. De'far . . ." swore Seppa, shaking his head.

"What do you mean? A peace has been made! With that Voidling?!" said the animated village head, his wispy beard swaying as he all but yelled. Clearly, the villagers did not like the idea of Del'more sticking around, Quinn thought. He, for one, did not blame them. Instead, he blamed only himself.

"Easy, friend," a soothing Samson said as he came in and put a reassuring hand on the village head's shoulder. "It's immortal, yes, but it's also trapped in the Deep Woods forever. If your people stay away from there, they'll be safe. Nothing has really changed for all of you in that regard. The Forbidden One's curse really has been lifted."

Whether it was Samson's solid argument or his naturally reassuring voice and demeanor, the village head and his council calmed visibly before them.

"Well, does that mean I still need to pay you? You didn't kill it. That means—"

"Killing it was never stipulated in the contract, friend," said an interrupting Fredstar on cue, his arms crossed and his mean, stern expression out on parade before the village elders. Fredstar was a man you didn't toy with.

Quinn and his brothers, watching from afar, smirked to each other at Fredstar's no-nonsense attitude to everything. How good it was to have him back with them was beyond words. Bells, how good it was to have them all back, Quinn thought before his self-condemnation kicked back in, causing him to look down then away from his smiling brothers' faces.

"Arghhh, I could really do with some drink right now," said Bryon, eyeing the small village establishment.

"He's right, dying makes a man thirsty," said Red with a smile as he followed the pub-bound direction the giant called Bryon was headed in.

"Come on Quinn. Drinks on us," said Michael before he too departed to join them.

"We owe you that much at least. Going one-on-one with that sentient Voidling. Bells, must have been a battle for the ages," said Lichale as he smiled lightly.

"Quinn, you alright?" said Tryan, asking a question he already knew the answer to from Quinn's downcast expression.

"I'll be fine. Just need some time to think," a not-fine Quinn said as he departed his worried-looking brothers, heading past the small village establishment called the Pothole to a place past the end of town, to where the swamp met a falling-away shoreline and a rotting dock. The words of Tar from a day ago still rang in his ears with every solemn step he took and every sway of his green forest cloak.

"As long as us Silver Serpents live, none shall speak the truth of what happened in the Deep Woods. We do this not to try and deceive anyone, but to protect ourselves against those who would misconstrue what happened there. If anyone learns that we were "dead" and that the Void may have brought us all back to life through unknown, perhaps twisted means, we'd be hunted and executed by the Akuan Guild within a week of them hearing about it.

"Or worse, an enterprising do-gooder like Madam Fayley of the Sirens might come for us instead. She wouldn't hesitate to burn us all alive, I'm sure. Men, I don't know what it means to die to oneself and, through forgiveness, be born again. But I do know this, that dead men have no tales to tell, and neither shall we."

And so this tale remained untold until I, Jest De'Blum of Narcass, pried it from Quinn's tight lips through the power of nagging. What really gets me though is had any member of those thirty families living in Parika' Te Mo bothered to keep a calendar (outside of the observance of nature around them), they would have eventually realized that their lives had seven days unaccounted for. But I digress; this story isn't over just yet.

***

Michael, Bryon, Tryan, Gus, Red, Seppa, and Lichale sat in eagerness as they watched a round of pints with their names on them head to their table. They slapped their knees and the wagon wheel table in front of them in anticipation of the liquid gold they were about to ingest. Each man, having felt they earned such a good cold brew ten times over, kicked back in relief. Each one feeling lucky to be able to enjoy one of life's oldest and humblest simple pleasures.

"Bells, that hits the spot," said Gus, having skulled the entire pint in one shot and now gesturing for a second.

"No offense, barman, but it tastes like watery shit," said Red as he eagerly went back for a second swig.

"I agree, but at the same time, it's the best pint I've ever had poured," said Lichale as all his brothers couldn't help but agree.

"It's because it tastes like life. Fresh and real, no pretension at all," said the quiet, scarred-face Michael, summing up the moment, beautifully in my opinion.

The barman shook his head dismissively. He did not truly understand what his Silver Serpent patrons were saying. Only that they were very tired, very weary men (as most Akuansmen are), who had come closer to death than they ever wanted to.

The Serpents went quiet for a while as they drank. As the roof leaked a drip of water into a bucket beside their haphazard table and the stools they rested upon, each man still struggled to

176

process what had happened during the likes of this unspeakable campaign. They did not truly understand what had happened to them, but they did understand this: their time in the Deep Woods had left them all a little changed. For better or worse? It remained to be seen.

As the celebration went on not in cheers of glory but in cheers of silent contemplation, they enjoyed the simple nothingness of the moment. That was, until an older man they had the unfortunate pleasure to have met, broke their silent celebration with sudden spoken word.

"You lot back then?" said Pell, the old fisherman in his fifties. The very one who first spoke the three-word title that every Serpent now naturally recoiled at the thought of. "Have ya lads done it then? Did you slay The Forbidden One?"

The men around the circular table just sat there in yet another bout of silence. Not wanting to answer the liar with words, each man instead answered with a blank expression as they looked back at him, still standing in the doorway of the pub.

"You don't want to know," said First Adjunct Samson as he surprised Pell by coming up behind him in the doorway. Seeing there were no stools left for him at the table with his Akuan, Samson came and sat at the bar beside Pell.

"Very well. I guess if you lot are still kickin' round, everything worked out with the Deep Woods. With that Voidling and all . . ." said Pell as he ordered a drink for himself at the bar. With a look of poorly hidden caution on his face, Pell acted like a man who was about to be unmasked as a bullshit artist at any moment. Were the Serpents onto him? Would there be fallout for his lies? Did he have them chasing a ghost in the Deep Woods this entire time? he likely wondered.

"Aye, it went well," said Tryan after a long silence from everyone.

Pell turned back to the group of Serpents, having received his drink. Pell then said with a grin as he began to do again the only

177

thing he was truly gifted at (bullshitting people) once more, "Well, you lot don't seem to be in a talkin' mood, but I am. Hey, now that I got you all here, how about another stor—"

"NO!" said all the men who sat at the wagon wheel table at once, breaking the silence and causing Pell to spill his drink a little from the sudden uproar.

"GOD NO . . ." fearfully grunted Gus. It was Pell's tall tale that created the monsters in their minds that Del'more used to kill them all. Even Pell was slain by a figment of his own imagination, though he did not remember it.

Samson leaned over on his barstool as Pell looked at the seated Akuansmen in bewilderment, a hint of fear on his face. Pell realized, yes, he had been found out as a liar. Worse still, by a bunch of highly trained Rogue Caster-killing men.

Samson, enjoying the humor of the situation, just grinned, then said to Pell plainly, "Let me give you some free advice, friend. Never, I say never, knowingly tell a tall tale again."

***

Quinn sat before a swampy shore, before a small dock that, with each passing month, grew a little greener with algae and plant growth. He, like his brothers in the pub, sat in silent contemplation of all the events that had transpired since he last sat there thirteen days ago.

Quinn looked back at the person he was all those days before and saw himself not as a man but as a naive child. A newly forged Akuansman dreaming of righteous purpose and steadfast brotherhood, not realizing that sometimes they would be contrary ideals.

Quinn looked at the swamp in front of him where Telligood had breathed his last. Its waters were murky and bile, just like the day he first found it. Made so by the natural processes of the swampy terrain around it, it had returned to its default state.

Telligood's final gift of pure waters had been completely corrupted with time. Quinn's head sank yet again. Would Quinn's pure gift of forgiveness to Del'more be thus corrupted? He earnestly wondered.

The frogs croaked from within the nearby reeds. The old man's bellow gently caressed the leaves of the trees all around him. A few splashes of alligators entering the water not far off were also heard in that peaceful moment among nature. It was only him and the clothes of our world for a while until he heard familiar-sounding footsteps behind him.

"I knew you'd be here, grieving your arse off when you should be celebrating with the men you sacrificed all for," Tar said as he walked up beside his probationary Silver Serpent, half telling him off. Quinn said nothing; he knew Tar was right but couldn't help himself.

He wanted to wallow in his own self-afflicted grief. He felt he needed to be punished. If not by others, then at least by himself. Ironically, he could forgive Del'more but not himself for what he viewed as sin.

Tar sighed loudly, fully wanting his tired mood to be heard as both men looked beyond the swampy shores at nothing in particular.

"There is an old saying: It's better to be judged by twelve than carried by six. Not sure if it applies in this circumstance . . . Maybe," Tar finally said. Quinn still did not have any words on the subject. So Tar sat down beside Quinn as he continued.

"To be honest, I knew that many of us would likely die in our attempt to kill the Forbidden One. From the very beginning, my gut said that this would be the contract that would finally do us all in. Yet I still took it up. You know why?"

"Because it needed doing?" Quinn said quietly, like he was only talking to himself.

"No, perhaps a little of that, yes. But mainly no. I took up this impossible task because I knew that whatever happened to

179

us, whatever we were presented with, you, my friend, would see the situation through justly. That you'd have the cold, logical heart to see something done even though it would cost you everything. That is the breed of man I thought you to be."

Quinn, feeling even more condemned at his mentor's words, let out a sigh then said, "Why'd you ever assume that?"

"Because that's exactly the way I am," said Tar, a half-smile on his face. "We are alike, you and I, Quinny. Not just in the fact we are both liars, mutants, living blades who pretend to not be prey. It goes beyond all that. To the extent that I thought us to share the same soul, which simply resides in two different bodies at the same time. That is, until three days ago."

"I disappointed you, sir."

"Yes, but perhaps in a good way. There are two kinds of mistakes in life. The mistakes you make for the right reasons and the mistakes you make for the wrong ones. Be glad you made the right sort of mistake. The one I can't condemn you for nor agree with."

"Sir. Are you really saying that I should have left you all dead? That to bring you back from death was a mistake?" Quinn asked earnestly, great concern on his face. Tar nodded.

"The damage has been done." Tar looked away from Quinn's face. "No use worrying about what could have been any longer. We must make the best of the future we have. The future is more valuable than the past, for it is still yet to be molded, changed."

"Does not the Fifth Oath say: Be kind to the stranger, the wayfarer, the unknown quantity along the journey. For good is rewarded with good, and absence of mercy is rewarded in turn. Does that not apply to Del'more?" Quinn rebutted, not satisfied with Tar's answer.

"Our Oaths do not apply to Voidlings. All Voidlings must be slain immediately as they come into our world. For they always bring chaos with them, even when they proclaim to come in peace. Our reality and that of the Void are like oil and water. They can never successfully mix." Tar stood up and walked over to the swampy shoreline, and Quinn then followed him there. Tar continued his lesson to Quinn.

"All we can do is remove said oil from this world the best we can; otherwise, our planet's entire fragile ecosystem will collapse . . . and us humans with it. To want to live in peace, that is a grand ideal. Worthy of heroic effort.

"However, to live in peace with something that is slowly killing you is like living with a disease you have the symptoms of but never treat until it finally kills. Del'more's continued presence in our world may not destroy it, but it slightly tips the balance in favor of our Armageddon, our end."

"Truly, must we slay all intelligent life that comes to us? Must we close our borders to beings from other worlds and other plains of existence forever?" Quinn asked, proving in that moment that naivety still lived in his wishful heart.

"Remember, my naive friend," Tar said smiling, "they already have a place to live, yet they choose to come to ours as invaders. We have no issue with them so long as they stay where they belong. I ask you, where will humans go once this world is made uninhabitable by creatures like Del'more? The answer is nowhere. We humans have only this world, this plane of existence. It isn't that we are closing our borders to the wider universe out of some ignorance like you infer. We close our borders because we wish to protect our only source of life in a totally hostile universe." Quinn nodded in affirmation. He understood the logic, but a part of him still didn't agree.

"You must understand, we humans are the beggars of the universe. We beg to be left alone," Tar said, summing up his point.

"And when looking poor and defenseless doesn't work for us, that's when we Akuans come in with the big stick," Quinn said seriously, which made Tar smile again.

"Exactly. My friend, my brother. It's okay to be wrong. I was wrong about who I thought you were; you were wrong about what you should have done. We still have that in common at least," Tar said in a good humor that stopped at Quinn's growing expression of despair.

"If it wasn't for you, Tar, getting us to believe in the seemingly impossible chance. Getting us to disregard what we felt and knew to be true in order to create an imagined hope that we could slay the Forbidden One. Without all of us believing, hoping as we did on the trek over there, that we could slay her, I'm sure I would have found Del'more as immortal as I am, simply because without your words of encouragement, we would have let our fears make her an obstacle unable to be bested. I only won because of you."

Tar slapped Quinn's back in a friendly gesture.

"And I only lost to Del'more because of you. Again, we are the same but slightly different."

Quinn fell to his knees at the shoreline. He all but wept from the emotional pain he felt in front of his mentor and confidant.

"But I couldn't go on without you all. The pain would have—"

"All pain ends; all suffering ends. Eventually," Tar said, this time without a smile, lost in his memories of the past. He purposely didn't look at Quinn's face as Quinn could no longer hold back his tears. "Do not worry, your pain will end one day. As it does for everyone."

"I do not weep because I feel only pain," Quinn said, surprising Tar with his sudden strong-willed voice. Quinn stood up. "I weep also because the man I idolized was not the man I thought he was."

Tar looked at Quinn, who stood taller than him but not by much.

"I cry because you sent us all to die. You would have sacrificed everything I live for to achieve one aim. That, in the grand scheme of things, does little to tip the balance in favor of anyone. You are not the man who our brothers revere and love."

"No, I'm a living blade, an Akuansman. We are not human, any of us. Just blades to be used then discarded in the war against the Void. Don't romanticize this. It's nothing but a numbers game, and I'm lucky to have a number in my Akuan that can be played more than once," Tar said with great seriousness.

"How can you live with that thinking?" Quinn said, almost in disgust.

"It's what you signed up for, isn't it? It's why we live free from kings and laws. Because each of us is already a dead man walking. We just haven't fallen into our graves yet."

"You sound like what I was fighting against; you sound a little bit like Del'more," said Quinn. Tar looked away, made uncomfortable by the thought.

"The Forbidden One is a chaotic neutral entity if ever there was one. I sense she neither wants to harm nor help anyone. She is only here for her own musings and to watch the suffering and fleeting joys of men. I am nothing like her."

"We are a source of entertainment for her. We are all a means to an end for you," said Quinn spitefully, looking down at the man he used to immortalize.

"Quinny, you don't see the full picture here. You don't understand the—"

"Then make me understand! Make me understand why exactly my brothers' lives had to be spent the moment you learned of the Forbidden One's existence here!" Quinn said in a rage. Tar just chuckled, shaking his head in disbelief at Quinn's pointed words.

"What you don't understand is this was all her plan!" Tar then yelled back, his anger finally finding him. "This entire exercise was relying on the fact that you would give into her evil. Remember what each of the Heralds said before they died? No?

Because I do! The first Herald, the child, said to us, 'If you believe in something, but it has no real effect on you, do you really believe it at all?' It was foretelling our crisis of confidence with those words before the Akuan experienced it."

Quinn stood, slightly taken aback. Still unsure of what Tar was saying, he shut up and listened.

"Next, the second Herald said, 'Another taken, another lost . . . Yet another toy broken, of human cost.' which foretold the way in which we were all picked off. One by one."

"Then when it said, 'Such pain . . . I feel pain . . .' it was not talking about itself?" said Quinn, thinking aloud.

"No, it was talking about you right now. I suspect that each Herald we found was actually Del'more in disguise. She was all three and none of the above at the same time. She is not a creature that has any form; she is like a spirit, an alien entity more akin to pure thought than anything."

"You are saying, sir . . . that I battled not a sentient Voidling but a collection of living thoughts? That need no body to contain them?" Quinn said, his mind blown. Tar nodded, his anger somewhat subsiding as he looked at the stillness of the swamp.

"This universe is a crazy place. Anything is possible within it."

"How did I not see this before?" Quinn said, still in shock. "Her power was to twist belief itself into a new reality. If Del'more is really just a group of sentient ideas, that just might explain how she did it all. She was not the Heralds; she was the curse that created them."

"It's worse still. Those sentient ideas that made it into this world through the gap in the Void can see into the future of everyone and everything here."

"And that is how she foretold what is happening now, back then. Is the Akuansmen's life always this complex?" Quinn asked earnestly, to which Tar just rolled his eyes.

"This world operates on a series of layers. The deeper you go, the more meaning can be found," Tar said, not particularly happy about that thought.

"Now that I really think about it, I followed the script laid out in Pell's tall tale perfectly. I had to 'discover the truth of the Deep Woods' to slay her once and for all."

"Yet you slew nobody. You made peace with her instead. You do realize that you let her win by that action."

"How so? It was a tie. Neither of us got what we fully wanted." Tar laughed dismissively at Quinn's earnest answer.

"You still don't see it. If she is as powerful as we think she is, if she could bring us back from the grave or whatever state of existence she held us in. If she could see our futures just as clearly as the present, perhaps even as clearly as the past, then surely whatever happened between you and her was of her devising alone. Quinny, she got everything she wanted from you."

Quinn lowered his head in guilt, and Tar took pity on him.

"Don't feel bad, you got played by the best. We all did."

"But that makes no sense," Quinn rebutted in disbelief. "She didn't get the land she wanted—"

"She never wanted land. She wanted an agreement with humanity, which you brokered in your desperation to see us again. She used the oldest trick in the merchant's handbook. She advertised her price higher than what she would have accepted, so you felt like you won something from her when you bargained her down.

"She was always willing to be trapped in the Deep Woods; her gaze likely extends beyond time and space itself. She never wanted the land. Likely, what she really wanted was to become alive in the thoughts of men by forming an accord, a right to exist in our realm. And now she has everything she wanted."

"I can't accept that," Quinn said, his tears drying up and a steadfast expression emerging on his face.

"Go on then, deny the truth," Tar said dismissively.

"I am simply doing what you yourself are."

"What?" Tar gave a look of confusion.

"You just tried to dodge my real question to you. Why did you want to spend our lives on this endeavor? Did you know from the start what the Forbidden One truly was? Bells, did you learn it from Sae's mind?"

"ENOUGH!" Tar shouted. Quinn had finally hit his target. "You'd be wise, probationary Serpent, to know when to hold your tongue about matters you know nothing about!"

"About secrets you still keep from me, of my past. Bells, you hold them over me like a dagger at my back sometimes. Will you betray my trust one day too as you did with my brothers?!"

Tar smacked the back of his hand against Quinn's face, breaking his fingers in the process from the force of the action alone. Quinn stood firm; he endured the blow undaunted.

"I'll give everything for these men! Everything I am, I give to these men!" Tar yelled as he slammed his chest with his broken hand, his emotions overcoming him. "The only thing I can't give them in this life is a peaceful death." Tar wept as Quinn too started to weep.

Finally understanding each other not through words but through their emotions, the two men embraced as they mourned openly. If there were any passersby at this point, they would have looked to Quinn and Tar and seen an elderly father and a young son.

"I want to tell you of your past, Quinny. Of what Sae, the real mastermind of this campaign against Del'more, told me that day before she left. Just before she gave me this impossible task. But I cannot; you are not ready for such truths, my brother. For they would destroy the man who chose to forgive instead of slay.

"Who chose to save instead of spend his brothers' lives against yet another one in a million Voidlings that need to be slain. The truth is, I thought you were just like me, a coldhearted, well-meaning machine of death. A living blade. But I see now you have the potential to be something else, someone else. Just like Sae described to me.

"That opportunity is something that Sae and I agreed was worth protecting above all else. I can't tell you why, but I was willing to sacrifice this Akuan, not to beat back the Void one more day. I was willing to sacrifice all because I thought it meant changing your fate. From the start, this was all about you alone."

"This was all an elaborate test of my character! What am I to you and Sae? That you'd do so much, go so far?" said Quinn as his voice waned.

"Quinny, I want to say but I can't. If I do now, everything will be undone. I must continue protecting you . . ."

"Protect me? But why? I'm immortal," Quinn said as they tore from their embrace and looked at each other.

With watery eyes, Tar said, "No, Quinn, you are not."

Chapter 14 – What We Are

The Silver Serpents took to their horses, glad at the thought they likely would never have to see this place again. The friendly people of Parika' Te Mo gathered en masse to see our heroes off. All the Serpents felt better within themselves. Due to a night's rest under a stable's solid roof, they felt civilized again.

"The Saints be with you, Silver Serpents," called out one of the many villagers gathered.

"May the roads be safe and open for ya," said one of the many fishermen in the crowd.

"The weather be light and the Voidlings scattered with the winds," said Pell, with a newly minted black eye, continuing the traveler's blessing with a smile on his face.

"The ale a plenty and the joy of life ever present," said the barman from the Pothole pub.

"May you bless others in life as we have blessed you," said the village head, finishing the traveler's blessing. Older than the stones in the Danneishie mountains, that blessing is said to be.

The Silver Serpents, with waves to the villagers, peeled off two by two in their usual traveling formation. Small children ran after them with laughter but soon gave up the chase when the Serpents passed the outer limit of the town.

Bells, they were finally free of the place, they all likely thought. After a while of cantering on their horses, the group slowed to a trot along the muddy dirt road.

"What's on our agenda, sir?" asked Fredstar as his horse trailed behind Tar, who took a lead position.

"Yeah, sir. Please tell us we are headed for a city. I could do with a good tavern's bed," said Tryan, yawning. He was always a man who overslept.

"Perhaps we should think of wintering early this year," suggested Samson, he too wanting some time away from the elements.

"Not yet, lads, not yet. The open road still beckons so long as snow hasn't fallen," Tar said with pride on his face as he twisted back in his saddle to look upon his grouped-up Akuansmen behind him.

"Yeah, slaying monsters. Not making peace with them like some people." Tryan made eyes at Quinn. "Sounds like there actually might be a profession in that," said Tryan. Everyone but Quinn chuckled. Tar smiled, then turned back in his saddle as Samson commented.

"You know, usually the hero of the tale kills the monster to bring about the conclusion of the story, but I kind of like this instead. It's unexpected. When was the last time, lads, that we left one alive and felt at rest about it?"

"Never. To my knowledge at least," grumbled Fredstar, happy for his life back but not about the means by which it was returned to him.

Lichale added to the thought by saying, "True. I have not heard any tale like ours. But I guess in the end, a hard-won peace is as satisfying an ending as any."

"Who are we? Storytellers? Bards?" asked Gus. "Why are we talking about this? We just got our shit kicked in by sentient fakkin' thoughts. And bloody worst of all, the trainee had to bail us out. Ruining the world a little bit as a result. Cause he forgot somehow that all Voidlings are purebred bastards for a bloody second. The kid's thick as they come, Tar; he might not be cut out for this," complained the loudmouth Gus as his brothers smirked at his half-serious mini tirade, Quinn included.

"How can a bastard be purebred?" questioned Tryan with a smile as Gus just ignored him and continued.

"Who are we, boss? I thought we were supposed to be Rogue Caster–killing bad arses or somethin'. You know, the ones lads everywhere wanna be but aren't because they are shite."

"Fakkin' oath mate, none of this forgive and forget our enemy bullshit," said Red. He and Gus forgetting they lacked this enthusiasm when it mattered most not long ago. Clearly, the loud and proud often have little underneath.

"Tar, what are we? Truly?" Quinn said, interrupting his senior brothers. Pushing Tar to speak the truth spoken in private between them just a few hours before, when Quinn asked this exact question.

Tar did not look back as he proclaimed, "We are not men, we are tools. We are called tools because men live by rules, and we do not. Does your bow bend due to man-made law? Does your sword cut through flesh because a man says it can? No. For us Serpents, all that we have to follow is the purpose that is illuminated on that ethereal plane where our hearts and heads meet. A normal human may be half animal, half God. But we are half human, half weapon of war. What are we, Quinny, you ask? We are all swords. Forged in the sufferings of life and made flawless in our duty and in our Oaths. Nothing less, nothing more. That is what it means to be a Silver Serpent. Del'more dead or not. In both victory and in loss, that is what we are."

"Hear, hear," said Second Adjunct Fredstar in an upbeat voice, prompting the rest of the men to confirm Tar's lofty words in the same way. That is, all men but Quinn.

Instead, he sunk his head low and did not utter a word. For he realized he did not yet live up to the Akuan's high-minded ideals. He was a blade, yes, but one without steadfast morals and considered action. His use of situational ethics when dealing with Del'more proved that to him, to them all.

If he was ever to become a full Silver Serpent like he wanted, like Tar and the rest of his Akuan brothers desired, he would have to develop his Oath-keeping, and in that, he still had a long way to go.

Afterword

I would like to thank you, dear reader, for taking this time out of your day to journey with me into both the heart of the Deep Woods and the ever-troubled Nameless Man himself. I set out in this tale to tell you a story that would unsequester for the Nameless Man a human face and reveal to all the heart of what he has always fought for—his adopted family. His Akuan.

Bells, I am ashamed to admit it, but during the course of gathering notes for this account, I went to see the being that is said to have tricked the Nameless Man into giving her peace, not cold steel like she rightly deserved. I too made my very own trek from Parika' Te Mo to the Deep Woods. You see, I thought I could go to Del'more as Quinn had; I thought in my great ignorance that I could get her to bring Quinn back from death. I believed and believed, and yet when I met her, Del'more said she could do nothing for him!

Bells, what I'd give to see my friend again in the flesh, not just in my somber memories. I feel now, as I finish writing this tale of Quinn, just as he would have felt when thinking of his Silver Serpent brothers lost forever. By the Saints, how I have come to know that unwanted burden. How I now understand why one would do absolutely anything to see such a weight lifted. I am envious of Quinn. I wish I could have now what he had then. If only for a moment, I would be able to be my old, chipper self again.

Alas, my meeting with the Forbidden One was far from entirely fruitless. Upon meeting her, I was surprised and heartened to learn that she no longer goes by the stolen name of Del'more Kar'dia. She goes now by the title the Nameless Man gave her. She calls herself the Woman of the Void. You've probably already heard of her.

Many foolish folk (myself included) travel to her realm in the Deep Woods, despite the many dangers, in an effort to seek out her otherworldly wisdom and visions of the past and future. Some even say she grants wishes, although she did not grant me my wish when I met her. The one I had to see my Akuan brother Quinn just one more time in the flesh.

You also are probably wondering why I am now going public with this account, considering its controversial nature, which might tarnish the Silver Serpent legend forever. Well, to those that think any less of the Silver Serpents because of my words, I say this.

In the end, the Silver Serpents won. Yes, you heard me. Recent history proves Quinn won the overall victory, not Del'more.

For I am gladdened to say that the Forbidden One really has changed from the being described in Quinn's account of her. Yes, she is still a devilish Voidling bent on laughing at humanity's woes. But to this day, she has only tricked not slain any mortals. Bells, even the town of Parika' Te Mo is comparatively safer these days.

All due to the Woman of the Void keeping the Void's filth in the Deep Woods where it belongs. I am proud to say that Quinn's counterattack of blind hope worked! Del'more became the Woman of the Void, the changed being Quinn hoped her to one day become. The pact Del'more made with the Nameless Man keeps to this day. Despite the fact that she no longer needs to fear the consequence of her breaking it.

For the immortal man called Quinn is no longer immortal at all. He has passed, proving that the inhuman monster many claimed him to be was, in the end, just as human as we all are. So there you have it. There is nothing more left to say, and so I shall end it here with a flourish, with a single thought neither Tar nor Quinn had considered during all the time they argued.

I say, to truly forgive someone of a wrong, you must first slay your offended self. What Quinn did was not selfish but self-sacrificing. A part of him died to save them all.